Frictional Characters

A Village Library Mystery

Elizabeth Spann Craig

Published by Elizabeth Spann Craig, 2022.

This is a work of fiction. Similarities to real people, places, or events are entirely coincidental.

FRICTIONAL CHARACTERS

First edition. February 8, 2022.

Written by Elizabeth Spann Craig.

Chapter One

I t was my day off from the library and I was blissfully sleeping in when my phone rang.

Instantly awake, I fumbled frantically for my phone as Fitz, the orange and white cat who spent his days at the library with me, blinked at me with concern. He was wondering why I had been curled up and sleeping one second and a mess of energy the next.

In my hurry to grab the phone, I knocked it clear off my bedside table. I scrabbled for it on the floor and then stared at it through sleep-blurred eyes. Wilson? Why was the library director calling me on my day off? Had I messed up? Was it *not* my day off?

"Wilson?" I said gruffly as I answered the phone right before it went to voicemail.

Wilson cleared his throat. "Sorry about calling you early on your day off. There's been . . . incident."

"An incident? What? Did something happen at the library?" My mind immediately flew to all kinds of horrible possibilities—a fire there. Tornado damage. A theft. Vandalism. I felt a little sick.

1

"No, no," he said quickly, seeming to understand my alarm. "I'm sorry, I'm not expressing myself very well this morning. I just found a body."

"What?" I croaked. "Where?" I had the sudden horror that it might be at the library.

"A body," said Wilson stiffly. "At Jonas Merchant's home . . . he's an acquaintance."

I stood up from the floor where I was still crouched with the phone. "You've called the police, though?"

"Yes, Burton and some others are here. In fact, they recommended that I call for a ride. I didn't want to alarm Mona."

Mona was the mother of my coworker, Luna, and the woman Wilson was dating. I said quickly, "I'll be over there as soon as I can. Do you have an address?"

Wilson said, "One second." He was quiet for a few seconds and then gave it to me. "Thank you, Ann."

I quickly got dressed and put some food out for Fitz before leaving. His happy purr rumbled to a quick stop as he started digging in.

I jumped into my old Subaru, plugged the address into my phone, and headed off down the street. It only ended up taking me a minute or two to get there. It was one of the short connecting streets that I took to the library every day. I might never even have noticed the name of it, or had definitely forgotten it if I had. When I drove up to the modest ranch house, I parked on the opposite side of the street because of all the emergency vehicles around.

Wilson was standing somberly on the sidewalk wearing his customary suit and tie, hands in his pockets. He'd gotten a bit more casual for a while, under Mona's influence, but old habits were hard to break and I was seeing him in his dark suits more often. He stiffly raised a hand in greeting and I gave a quick one back. I saw that our police chief, Burton—a big, middle-aged man—was speaking with some other police that must be from the North Carolina state police force. He glanced my way and nodded his head in greeting.

I walked up to Wilson. "Are you all right?"

Wilson nodded, although he seemed exhausted, despite the early hour. "I'm fine. But I'm not positive I can leave yet. I'd rather have Burton come over and okay my departure before I make it."

"Sure. I don't have anywhere I need to be. What happened?"

Wilson gave me a pained expression and then moistened his lips as if they were dry. "All I can say is that I had nothing to do with this, Ann."

"Of course you didn't." I hesitated. "Can you tell me why you're over here? Did you have business with Jonas?"

Wilson said sharply, "I've said all I can really say about it. All I want to do is to finish speaking with Burton and then head to the library. Here comes Burton now." He squared his shoulders as if ready to face some sort of firing squad instead of the kind-faced police chief.

Wilson flinched a bit as Burton gave him a pat on the back. But he managed to give the chief a strained smile.

"Holding up okay?" asked Burton.

"I suppose so," said Wilson miserably. He ran a hand through his white hair, making it stand uncharacteristically up on end. "Although I would frankly prefer to go home and back to bed. Perhaps I could start this day over again and have the outcome turn out better."

Burton gave him a small smile. "That would be a nice option to have, wouldn't it? And one a lot of people would want to try. I appreciate that you called us as soon as you found Jonas. But you've got to know, Wilson, it doesn't really look really great that you're not giving us more of an explanation as to why you're here. You've said that you and Jonas weren't friends."

Wilson looked repelled by the idea. "Certainly not."

Burton shrugged. "Then you must realize it looks strange that you were inside Jonas's house and found him."

Wilson stood stiffly, his expression unyielding. "I've said all I wanted to say on the matter."

Burton sighed, looking over at me with a frustrated look. "Okay. But you should know that's not going to be the end of it. We'll be in touch if there's anything else we need."

Wilson gave a stiff bob of his head, looking relieved. "Excellent. Thanks, Burton."

The police chief was called away and joined the forensic team at the front of the house.

"Ready to get out of here?" I asked quietly.

Wilson nodded again.

I walked over to my Subaru and hopped into the front seat. Wilson looked drawn and tired, in keeping with the early hour.

"Wilson, I was thinking that maybe you and I should go grab some breakfast."

He looked at me with an owlish expression. "It's very late, though. I should be getting to the library. I know I mentioned going back to bed, but I was just being facetious."

I shook my head. "There's really no reason to head into the library. It's fully-staffed today and no one needs any direct supervision. It's not the day for you to meet with the board of trustees. Besides, I'm sure you've built up plenty of time off." In all my days of working at the library, I couldn't immediately recall Wilson taking any vacation days.

For a second, he looked stubborn but then sighed. "I suppose you're right. I could use a little time to get my head screwed on straight. I just don't know if I feel like sitting out in public right now. I'm feeling a bit shaky. And I'm not sure I have any breakfast food at my house right now."

"Why don't you come by my place?" I asked. "It won't be as fancy as a restaurant, but I can definitely scramble us some eggs and fix coffee and toast."

Wilson relaxed a little. "That sounds perfect. As long as I'm not messing up any of your plans, Ann. I know today is supposed to be your day off. You surely didn't intend to spend it with the library director."

"It's my pleasure," I said quickly. I drove us back to my cottage where Fitz was sleepily blinking at us out of the front window.

Wilson chuckled. "It looks like you have a welcoming committee."

Sure enough, Fitz happily wound himself around Wilson's legs and then hopped into his lap as I busied myself in the small kitchen with making the aforementioned eggs, toast, and coffee. I gave him a steaming cup of coffee first, putting the half and half and sugar in front of him while I got the eggs and toast started. I sensed that Wilson felt a bit awkward about everything that had happened so I kept busy with the cooking and Fitz kept Wilson busy by loving on him.

I realized as I was cooking that I hadn't eaten breakfast, myself. I put a couple of extra eggs in the pan. When I put the food down on the kitchen table and joined Wilson, I was pleased to see that his color looked better. He took a few bites of eggs and toast and then sat back in his chair a little, reaching down to rub Fitz again.

"I can't imagine what you must be thinking, Ann," said Wilson sadly. "I hope the events of the morning haven't changed the way you think about me."

"I always have total respect for you," I said immediately. It was true. Wilson could irritate me sometimes, especially when he loaded me up with extra work. But he worked just as hard and cared so much about what we did at the library. And he'd always conducted himself with so much integrity.

He sighed with relief. "I'm so glad to hear that. Thank you for not pressing me on the matter." He hesitated. "You seem to have a natural talent for solving these types of puzzles. It must be a good trait for a librarian to have. Maybe you can do some digging for me . . . figure out who might be responsible for Jonas's death. I just hate that the trustees might think I'm a murderer."

"Of course they won't," I said stoutly. "Anyone who knows you will realize you're completely incapable of harming anyone."

"Thanks," said Wilson, although he sounded doubtful. He finished off his coffee and said, "And now I think I should get out of your hair for the day."

"Are you feeling any better?" I asked.

He nodded. "A lot. The food and caffeine have done their jobs."

He did look a good deal better and he said he thought he'd be able to drive again. So I dropped him off back at Jonas's house where his car was parked. The emergency vehicles were still there and police officers were continuing to go in and out of the house and consulting each other in small groups in the yard. Wilson carefully avoided the scene with his eyes.

I got out of the car too, mainly just to make sure Wilson walked over to his car okay. I heard my name being called and turned around.

Chapter Two

I saw a beautiful woman in her thirties with dark hair coming toward us. I waved to her. Flora was someone I'd come to know as a friend. When I'd inherited the cottage from my great-aunt, I'd felt overwhelmed by the lush landscaping at the house. But my aunt had dearly-loved her garden and had felt so much pride in it that I knew I had to keep it up. Flora, who was a master gardener, was a lifesaver. Afterwards, we kept up with each other's lives with an occasional coffee and whenever Flora came over to the library—which had become more and more frequent. Unfortunately, Flora was also Jonas's sister and it looked as if she might not know the news about what happened.

Wilson murmured, "One of our regular patrons at the library, I believe."

"That's right," I quietly responded. "Flora Merchant."

Wilson suddenly looked very uncomfortable. "Jonas's sister. Oh no. She looks as if she hasn't heard."

"I guess there hasn't been enough time for Burton to get over there and speak with her." My stomach twisted at the thought.

Sure enough, Flora was looking very confused. "Hi, Ann. Do you know what's going on here at this house? My brother lives here."

I gave her a quick hug in greeting and said cautiously, "I think you should speak with Burton, Flora. He's right over there with some other police at the front door. He'll know more about what's happening than I do."

But Flora was having none of it. She wanted to know right then what had happened. "He's dead, isn't he? My brother. Why else would they have a team in forensics suits?" Her voice was quiet but insistent.

Wilson gave me a stressed look. I cleared my throat and said as gently as possible. "I'm afraid he is, Flora. Would you like to take a seat in my car?" I pushed open my car door as far as I could and Flora sat down hard on the seat. Her face was bemused.

"What happened?" she asked.

Wilson and I looked at each other again and I caught Burton's eye and waved him to come over. He gestured to indicate he'd be there as soon as possible.

Wilson said carefully, "We don't really have a lot of information right now. But from what I gathered from speaking with Burton earlier, it seems to have possibly been foul play."

Flora looked grim and surprised but not exactly grief-stricken. "Sounds like karma," she muttered with a short laugh. Then she looked up at both of them. "Sorry, that must sound awful. I cared about Jonas, of course. He was my big brother. But he could be a really difficult person and caused a lot of trouble sometimes. I can see where someone might have become really upset with him."

Burton joined them as Wilson slipped away to head to his car. Burton spoke quietly to Flora, giving her basic information about Jonas's death and telling her how sorry he was. When he saw how composed Flora remained, he cautiously began asking a few questions. "Have you spoken with your brother this morning? Did he perhaps ask you to come over?"

Flora shook her head. "Nothing like that. I was just driving by his house on my way to work—I just stopped when I saw all the emergency vehicles here. Jonas and I didn't keep in touch as well as we should have."

"I was wondering if you might be able to give a little information about your brother. Could you fill me in with a bit of background?"

Flora squared her shoulders as if facing a somewhat unpleasant task. "I'm happy to help out, if I can. As I mentioned, I'm afraid Jonas and I weren't particularly close, but I have known him for a long time."

Flora seemed very calm and composed. I knew her as someone who was always very practical and who had a great deal of equilibrium, but it was a little startling how unfazed she was by her brother's sudden death.

"What was he like?" asked Burton.

Flora sighed. "I was just saying to Ann and Wilson that my brother could be a very difficult man. He was always very smart growing up but seemed lazy—he wouldn't hand in his assignments on time or even finish some of them. I got the feeling he was the same way in the working world. He was always looking for shortcuts to avoid doing a lot of work."

Burton slowly asked, "Was he ever on the wrong side of the law?"

Flora nodded, coloring a bit with embarrassment. "I'm afraid so, although it's been ages ago. He would always want to make a quick buck instead of sitting for hours in an office to make it legitimately. He was arrested once, probably ten years ago, for minor fraud charges. I had to bail him out of jail, which is the only reason I know about it. We never discussed it after that."

Burton asked, "But he did have a regular job here in Whitby, didn't he?"

Flora gave a short laugh. "Yes. He was an insurance agent. Although I'm not sure he was very motivated at the office. He wasn't the kind to fall all over himself to sell you a policy. And I'm not positive a client could depend on Jonas to answer the phone if they did have an accident."

"The house—this used to be your father's house, didn't it? Is he now in a retirement home?"

Flora shook her head. "He died, unfortunately."

"And Jonas was bequeathed the house?"

I remembered that this was something of a sticking point for Flora. We'd had some casual chats together when she'd complained about Jonas. He'd not been helpful taking care of their father and yet he'd ended up with their father's property.

Flora took a deep breath. "Well, he thought Jonas was the perfect son. I guess Jonas seemed that way . . . he sure was super-attentive on the phone once a week." Her voice was bitter.

I said quietly, "But you were super-attentive, yourself. You were taking care of your father."

Flora lifted her chin. "That's right. I was his caretaker. But Dad was very old-fashioned and thought that it was my duty to care for him. He didn't really appreciate it that much. That's why he left his house to Jonas instead of me." She shrugged. "It was okay. I don't know why I was expecting anything more. Jonas moved down here just as soon as he was given the house."

Burton lifted an eyebrow. "That must have made you upset. Considering how much work you'd done for your father and how much help you'd given him throughout the years."

Flora shrugged. "I think it was because my father got irritated with me. I spent so much time with him that I got on his nerves. I was always pushing him one way or another . . . to make a doctor appointment or do his PT exercises or something like that. Over the years, he likely got fed up with it. I think he must have made the change to his will in the middle of all that."

"And Jonas never tried pushing your dad? Or was engaged in his care at all?" I asked.

Flora gave them a weary look. "No. He couldn't be bothered." She glanced at her watch. "I'm sorry—I need to tell work that I'm going to be late."

Burton said, "You might want to take the day off, Flora. This is a lot to wrap your head around. And there will likely need to be some planning involved for the next steps."

Flora sighed. "You're right. It's just if I don't work, I don't get paid. It's not exactly a salaried job." She made a quick phone call to let them know. Wilson excused himself and sat in my car's passenger seat out of earshot.

After she'd hung up, Burton said, "Could you just fill in for me your activities for the last twelve hours or so?"

Flora considered this. "Well, I was at my apartment last night after working yesterday. I stayed there all night and this morning until I arrived here. I was at home with my cat. And she's not much of an alibi." Flora frowned. "Oh gosh. Jonas's dog. I can take him for you, if that works."

Burton looked relieved. "Can you? That would be great. My deputy has him on a leash in the backyard right now. I'll let him know after we're done talking." He paused. "Do you know if you'll be taking possession of the house at some point?"

"I have no idea if Jonas had a will or if I am even in it," said Flora in a weary voice. "There's just no telling with him. We don't have any other relatives, though, and Jonas never married. He has no children. If he doesn't have a will, I guess it's going to take forever to go through probate court. But I suppose I may end up with the house." She took a deep breath as if bracing herself for something. "Could you please tell me what you know about his death? And why you think it was foul play?"

Burton pressed his lips together and then said carefully, "Flora, I wish I could tell you all about it right now. But the fact of the matter is that we're going to have to investigate more and let forensic results come in before we get a better picture. All I can tell you right now is that he was struck on the head with a heavy object. His death definitely wasn't accidental."

Flora nodded her head, looking tired.

Burton continued, "Do you have any idea who might have wanted to harm your brother? Did Jonas ever speak to you about issues he was facing? Trouble with other people?"

Flora quietly considered this. She said slowly, "Jonas did mention that he'd been irritated with his neighbor. Or maybe that his neighbor was irritated with him—I can't really remember."

Burton jotted down another note. "Any idea what the trouble was about?"

Flora snorted. "Well, I know it had more to do with Jonas than with his neighbor. Reggie, I think his neighbor is."

I must have made a sign of recognition because Burton asked me, "Do you know Reggie, Ann?"

"Maybe. I know a Reggie who comes into the library regularly, anyway. And it's not a very common name."

"That's probably him," said Flora. "I think he's an academic of some kind. As far as what the trouble was about, I think it had something to do with the awful state of the yard. I'm going to have to do something about it right away, if I'm to be responsible for it. When Dad was alive, he could at least afford to pay a small amount for a kid to cut the grass every week during the summer. Jonas didn't care much about that kind of stuff, though. And Jonas's dog tends to bark a lot when he's left outside."

Burton said, "I'm guessing Jonas wasn't the best pet owner, either?"

"Exactly. He tended to neglect the poor animal. I feel just awful about it." Flora snapped her fingers. "And there was one other thing. One of Jonas's trees fell down into Reggie's yard, crushed his fence, and Jonas refused to pay for its removal, even though it was his tree."

Jonas did sound like a complete nightmare of a neighbor.

"Anyone else?" asked Burton.

Flora hesitated. "I know that Jonas recently ended a relationship with a woman. I don't really know her well. Her name is Augusta Weber. Considering the fact that Jonas could be rough around the edges, it's possible that she might have been resentful about the way he ended things. I got the feeling it was pretty abrupt."

Burton jotted down a couple more notes. "Thanks for all this, Flora." He lowered his voice a little. "Is that the neighbor there?"

Sure enough, there was a young man, probably about my age, who was standing not far away and looking very curious. He was the patron I'd guessed he was. Flora glanced in his direction and I saw him smoothing his hair down and giving her a shy smile.

"That's Reggie," Flora confirmed. She glanced at her watch again. "Is there anything else I can help you with, Burton? I hate to cut it short, but I should get on to work."

Burton shook his head. "No, I think that's all for now. Again, I'm really sorry, Flora. Maybe you should just work a partial day and try to take things easy. I'll be in touch if I have any additional questions."

She gave him a smile and then hurried back to her car. Burton smiled at Reggie and gestured him over. Reggie's smile faltered but he hurried in our direction.

Chapter Three

"Hi Ann," he said, with that smile again. "Sorry for butting in," he said automatically. "I just wanted to make sure everything was all right or to see if I can help." He hesitated. "What's happened?"

Burton said solemnly, "I'm afraid your neighbor has died."

Reggie's blue eyes opened wide. "Jonas? Wow. I mean, I'm sorry to hear that."

I noticed that Reggie did seem surprised, but not particularly heartbroken at the news of his neighbor's demise.

"How was Jonas as a neighbor?" asked Burton.

Reggie shifted a bit uncomfortably. "As a neighbor?" He seemed to be at a bit of a loss for words.

"That's right. Just a general picture of him. You lived right next door so I'm guessing you have some thoughts. Was he tidy? Quiet?"

This seemed to strike a chord in Reggie and he gave a short laugh. "I'm afraid he was neither tidy nor quiet."

Burton turned a page in his tiny notebook and nodded. "So things changed a bit when Jonas moved in after his father died."

16

"That's right." Reggie cleared his throat and looked uncomfortable. "Look, I don't really want to throw the man under the bus, especially if he's dead now."

Burton looked up. "Actually, it would be a huge help for me. I'm trying to put together a ~~together~~ _picture_ of him."

"Well, I'm not sure I'm the right person to help with that. I mean, I barely knew him."

Burton said, "What the investigators will do is to construct a picture of Jonas from the recollections of many different people. It's an invaluable tool for us as we try to piece together what happened."

Reggie slowly nodded. "I'm gathering this must have been a suspicious death."

"We're treating it that way until we have further information," said Burton in a noncommittal voice.

Reggie took a deep breath. "All right. In that case, I'll tell you what little I know. I feel terrible about his poor dog. I mean, it drove me completely insane by barking all day. But it needed attention and love. I blamed Jonas for that, not the dog." He frowned. "What's going to happen to it now?"

Burton said, "Jonas's sister is taking him in."

At the mention of Flora, Reggie flushed a little. "Is she? That's good. Like I said, I felt sorry for him. Just the same, it was very difficult to work from home. I'm a professor and I'd be trying to read essays and the barking wouldn't help."

Burton jotted down a few notes. "I understand there may have been issues with the yard, too?"

Reggie looked surprised that Burton knew this.

"Small towns," said Burton with a smile.

"Yes," said Reggie. He seemed to consider his words carefully. "Well, unfortunately, Jonas didn't do much to maintain the yard after he took over the house. It really wasn't a problem when his father lived here because he had a yard service come over to mow and clip the bushes and whatnot. But now?" He nodded at the long crabgrass.

"There might have been an issue over a tree, as well?"

Reggie looked a little flustered. "Yes. It wasn't a huge deal, but the fact of the matter was that it was Jonas's tree. Not only did it do some damage to my fence, but he absolutely refused to pay for the tree's removal. And I'm not exactly made of money, you know. It had a significant impact on my bank account."

Burton jotted down a couple of notes. "Could you just fill me in as to where you were last night and this morning?"

Reggie's face went from flushed to ashen. "You don't think I had anything to do with this, do you?"

"It's just standard procedure," said Burton easily.

Reggie stammered out, "I don't have an alibi. Alibis are the sort of thing innocent people don't have. I was doing some grading and preparing for a lecture yesterday evening and this morning. I had my earbuds in and was listening to music."

"You didn't leave the house."

"No! Well, maybe just to take a walk at one point, but it was a short one." Reggie was gazing anxiously at Burton.

"Did you see or hear anything unusual next door? See anyone arriving at the house?"

Reggie shook his head. "I was deeply engrossed in what I was working on. I made a lot of progress because I was focused on my work. Aside from the quick walk to clear my head, that is."

"What subject do you teach?" asked Burton. I suspected he was trying to put Reggie at ease since he was looking more and more wound up.

"History," said Reggie, clearing his throat nervously.

"What do you think of the school?" asked Burton, still in that casual voice.

Reggie loosened up a bit and spent a few minutes talking about the beautiful campus, the amiable faculty, and the excellent students they had. Then he abruptly stopped, his gaze drifting toward Jonas's house as more police entered the building.

He said, "Jonas wasn't all bad, though. He kept to himself, but I was fine with that. It's just those issues that I outlined. I suppose they really weren't all that important, really."

Burton said, "I'm surprised you didn't call me to mediate the problem."

Reggie raised his eyebrows. "Is that what people do?"

"All the time," responded Burton wryly. "It's a small town. They know I'm not ordinarily working on a big case."

Reggie said, "I tried to fix the problem by speaking reasonably to Jonas. I didn't want to escalate things because I had the feeling that Jonas was going to be in that house for a long time. I didn't want the stress of having a neighbor who was furious with me."

"How did Jonas respond when you tried to speak calmly with him?"

Reggie gave a short laugh. "He was a real jerk, honestly. Especially about the dog. I mean, I'm a dog owner myself and I can't imagine neglecting an animal that way. And he showed no indication of feeling responsible about either the dog or his property."

"Do you have any idea who might have wanted to harm Jonas?" asked Burton. "Did you happen to notice him having any disagreements with anyone else?"

Reggie considered this. "I saw him have an argument with a man just a couple of days ago. I don't know who the guy was, though."

"You'd never seen him over there before?"

Reggie shook his head. "But I might be able to describe him a little. He reminded me of someone I used to know, but it's definitely not the same guy. He was average height, had a bushy black mustache and sort of a grim, taciturn expression."

To me, the description sounded just like Ted Hill, the owner of the local garage.

Burton jotted down a few notes. "Okay, got it. Did you happen to notice what type of vehicle he was in?"

"An old Ford truck. I was just coming back from the college when he was over there. I couldn't help but look over there because the guy was very angry and had his voice raised."

"Could you hear what he was saying?" asked Burton.

"Not really." Reggie frowned. "Something about his sister."

"About Jonas's sister or the man's sister?"

Reggie said, "The man's sister. It sounded like Jonas might have been harassing the sister or something because the guy was telling him to leave her alone." He shrugged. "I'm sorry. That's all I've got."

Burton carefully recorded Reggie's words, looking troubled. "Thanks for your help. I think that's all I need for now."

Reggie departed with an air of relief.

"I should head out, too," I said.

Burton nodded. "Thanks for helping out with Wilson." He sighed. "I don't suppose Wilson gave you any indication why he might have been over here this morning."

I shook my head. "He wouldn't say a word about it."

Burton rubbed the side of his head. "It just doesn't look really good, Ann. He was over at Jonas's house, won't tell us why, then found his body. He sure seems like a major suspect."

"But he also was the one who called you. He could have just left the house and no one would have been the wiser. Plus, it's *Wilson*. He's probably the most upright citizen in town."

Burton said, "I know. Just let me know if he spills something to you. All I've got right now for suspects is a sister who might have wanted to inherit a dilapidated house and a guy who might or might not have had a dispute over a dog and a tree. It sure doesn't add up to much." He paused. "Do you have any ideas as to who that guy was who Reggie was describing?"

I nodded. "It sure sounded like Ted Hill."

Burton's eyes lit up. "The mechanic?"

"Well, he's actually the owner of the shop, but yes."

Burton said, "Can I give you some information that can't go any further?"

I nodded and he continued, "The weapon was a half-inch torque wrench. Someone had tossed it in Jonas's garage to make it look like it was just one of Jonas's tools. Our forensics guys realized it was the weapon."

My eyes widened a little.

"Could you give me a little information on Ted?" asked Burton.

I said slowly, "Well, I don't know him very well, of course. He's just the guy everyone pretty much takes their cars to in town. He's quiet, kind of gruff. He runs a tight ship over at his garage, I think. He seems like the kind of guy who doesn't put up with a lot of nonsense."

"Do you know if he knew Jonas? It sure seems like he came by here, according to what Reggie was saying. Or if Ted might be capable of doing something like this?"

I shook my head. "I don't, sorry."

Another cop called him away and he gave me a quick wave and hurried back to Jonas's house.

Since I was already out, I decided to run the couple of errands I had. I went by the post office, picked up a prescription at the pharmacy, and then hesitated. After speaking with Flora earlier, I had the sudden desire to go by the garden center. I sighed. I'd been wanting to spruce up the flowers around my mailbox for a while and the conversation with Flora just reminded me about it again. Hopefully, Flora wouldn't think that I was stalking her.

I was relieved when Flora, who was watering plants, raised a hand in greeting when I walked in a few minutes later.

"It's a lovely day to do some planting," said Flora with a smile.

"Isn't it? When I was with you earlier, I was suddenly in the mood to work on my garden. The ones I put out got too much sun and not enough water." I grimaced. "Clearly, I made some bad choices."

"I can give you some suggestions, if you'd like," suggested Flora, putting down the hose she was using.

I nodded, relieved. I didn't have the money to invest in bad flower choices and having an expert would make all the difference.

Soon my cart was filled with yarrow, black-eyed Susans, and a daylily. Flora was cheerful and informed and it was impossible to tell that she'd just lost her brother unexpectedly.

Flora seemed to realize her demeanor was at odds with the events of the day. She gave a short laugh. "It's been a very odd day. Sort of surreal."

"I feel that way too, and I didn't even know him. I'm sorry—you must be experiencing a lot of different emotions."

Flora sighed. "I am. Clearly, it's obvious that Jonas and I weren't close. We didn't have a lot in common . . . even when we were kids. He was really motivated by money and I just want a simple life. But I still cared about him, of course. I think the overwhelming feeling I'm having is one of guilt. I feel like I should have been a better sister to him—maybe been more of an ear for him. Who knows—he might still be alive."

I said, "I think it's only natural to feel a sense of guilt when someone close to us dies. But Jonas's death was not your fault, Flora." I hesitated. "There are some really helpful books at the library that might be useful for helping you get through this. I know they helped me when my great-aunt died. I'd be happy to pull them out for you the next time you're at the library."

Flora smiled at me. "That would be great. I've got to run by there soon anyway to return some books. And I need something to distract me from all this. While I've been working, I keep thinking about who could have wanted to harm Jonas. And it didn't help that Burton called me right when I was finally starting to get my head into taking care of the plants."

"Burton called?"

"That's right. He was asking me about Hattie Gray. Is she someone you know?"

I nodded. "I know her from the library. She comes by several times a week to get work done after school—she's the principal at the high school."

"I see. I don't know her at all and told Burton that. Apparently, one of the neighbors mentioned having seen her at Jonas's house." She sighed. "I definitely got the feeling that none of the neighbors were fans of Jonas's."

Considering this sounded like a tip from *another* neighbor, not Reggie, I had to agree. "How's the dog doing?"

Flora smiled. "Pretty well, actually. I was amazed Bandit settled in so well at my house. I set out some water and the cops handed me some of the dog food Jonas had in the house and a couple of bowls. I thought he might start crying when I left to come to work, but he was quiet as a mouse—just curled up on some towels I laid on the floor and went right to sleep."

I walked with Flora to the cash register and paid for the plants. We chatted about other things for a couple of minutes and then I headed back home. I put on some yard clothes and old shoes and took out a shovel and a spade to plant the flowers around the mailbox. Fitz watched with interest from the front window, casually bathing himself from time to time.

Of course, I'd picked the hottest time of the day to do my planting. I accidentally smeared dirt on my face as I absently reached up to push a strand of black hair out of my eyes.

"I thought this might come in handy," said a voice behind me. I turned with a smile to see my boyfriend, Grayson, reaching out a hand with a water bottle in it.

"Thanks," I said and took a few gulps of the cool water. "I don't know what I was thinking, doing this digging in the middle of the day."

"If I know you, and I'm starting to, I think you were just knocking things off your to-do list as quickly as possible." Grayson's eyes crinkled at the edges in that way I loved.

I chuckled. "You're right about that. I'd thought I might relax a little today, but apparently, relaxing isn't in the cards."

Grayson said, "It's your day off so you get to choose how to spend it."

I answered wryly, "Do I? I'd have thought that was the case, but my day got hijacked pretty early."

He frowned. "Early? It didn't have anything to do with that mysterious death in your neighborhood, did it?"

Grayson, the local newspaper editor, naturally had quite an ear for any local story. "I'm afraid it did. There's not much I can say about it, though, unless we're speaking off the record."

"Of course we are," he said immediately. "Are you okay? Did you know the deceased? Jonas was his name, I think?"

"I didn't really know him, no. I did see his father from time to time. But Wilson had some business with Jonas—I can't really elaborate more than that—and discovered Jonas's body. As you can imagine, he was pretty shaken up."

Grayson gave a low whistle. "He must have been. So . . . did he call you?"

"He did. He'd driven over to Jonas's house and didn't feel confident about driving afterwards. I brought him by here for a little while and we had breakfast together. He was better by the end." I paused. "Do you know much about Ted Hill?"

Grayson raised his eyebrows. "Are we still on the subject of Jonas's death?"

"Sort of. Ted Hill might have had something of a run-in with Jonas and I'd like to find out more about it. Plus, between you and me, Wilson worries he might be considered a suspect in Jonas's death. He thought I might be able to casually dig around a little and see what I might be able to find out."

"You're good at that," said Grayson. "Just be careful. And I do know Ted Hill, but only because he owns the tire and auto shop that I go to." He paused. "As a matter of fact, I've been putting off an oil change for my car for the last couple of weeks. You could come along with me for a good excuse to talk with him. Casually, like you said."

"Do you have time to do that this morning? Sorry about the rush. Wilson was just so shaken up that I feel sort of personally invested. I know you're working today."

He grinned at me. "Considering this information may help with the biggest local story the paper has right now, I think I can spare the time. And I might be able to make Ted a little chattier than he is ordinarily."

"Is he not usually a chatty person?"

Grayson said, "I think the word to describe Ted is *taciturn*."

"Well, that's definitely not helpful," I said dryly.

"Yeah. But I have hopes of getting him to open up a little. Are you ready to head out now?"

I was. I gave Fitz a rub and he curled up happily in a sunbeam as I headed out to the tire and auto shop with Grayson.

Chapter Four

I was familiar with the auto shop because it was really the only place in town to get work on your car done. I knew the shop had been in Ted's family for at least a couple of generations. It was a brick building with an old painted sign that announced "Hill's Auto" in staid lettering. Ted himself was rather staid, I thought, but then I hadn't tried to get him to really open up the few times I'd been over to the shop. I'd been more intent on reading my book in his waiting room.

But Grayson greeted Ted as if he were a long-lost friend, giving him a hearty handshake and grin. Ted, with his oil-stained hands, looked rather bemused but not displeased to see him. "Good to see you," he said gruffly.

"Just an oil change today. I'm afraid it's pretty long overdue but at least I'm getting to it. Do you know Ann Beckett, Ted?"

Ted peered at me and said, "Subaru?"

I blinked at him. "Wow. You have an incredible memory. I don't think I've brought the car by here as often as I should have."

Ted looked pleased by the compliment. "Sometimes I remember cars better than people."

"I'm sure you hear a lot of gossip in a place like this, too, don't you?" said Grayson. "Did you hear about Jonas Merchant?"

Ted gave him a sharp look. "As a matter of fact, I did. But I'd like to hear your take on what happened to Jonas." His lip seemed to curl a little bit as he spoke and I noticed he didn't seem to deny knowing Jonas, even though Jonas hadn't been in town for very long.

Grayson looked over at me. "Ann might know more about it than I do right now." I quickly filled Ted in while he shook his head.

"What's the world coming to?" he said finally. "Although I can't say I cared for the man. He was worse than useless—he was toxic." He paused. "The reason I know about Jonas's death isn't because of gossip. The police came by here a little bit ago."

I raised my eyebrows. That was fast work on Burton's part.

Ted sighed. "If I'd known I needed an alibi, I would have gotten that sorted out. But I didn't. I've been spending a lot of time here at the shop, but it's been before hours so no one else can verify that. The cops didn't seem to be able to even give me an exact time of death." He looked at us. "Do you know?"

Grayson and I shook our heads.

Ted continued, "I've been doing some accounting for the business and it's taking up a good deal of time since I'd put it off for a while. I'm not sure the cops believed me, though. You never know with them."

Grayson said, "Do you know why the police wanted to speak with you? It doesn't sound like you were very close to Jonas."

Ted snorted. "No, I wasn't. And the cops didn't really give me much information. They just said something at the crime scene was a connection to me. I have no idea what it could have been. Anyway, Jonas was total and complete scum, so his death was no great loss. I've heard all kinds of stories about him."

Grayson and I must have looked curious because he gruffly added, "I'm not going to repeat them here since I don't like gossip. Let's just say that Jonas was the lowest of the low. He didn't deserve to exist. I take my hat off to whoever did him in. But it wasn't me."

He glanced away from me but as he did, I thought I caught a glimmer in his eye. Did Ted know who killed Jonas? Or maybe just have his suspicions?

I said, "I haven't spent too much time around him, myself."

Ted snorted. "Well, you've done yourself a favor."

The door behind them opened and another customer came in. Ted raised his hand in a greeting. He quickly said, "I've gotta go. Your car will be ready in fifteen minutes." He stepped out into the bay.

After the oil had been changed in Grayson's car, he drove me back to the house. "What have you made of all this so far?"

"I don't really know what to think," I said. "Flora, Jonas's sister, is a friend of mine and I just can't see her having anything to do with her brother's death. Her family must be important to her because she sacrificed a lot of years taking care of her father. Although I know she and Jonas weren't very close."

Grayson said, "I'm pretty surprised to hear Wilson was caught up in it all."

I answered a bit more sharply than I'd planned. "He's not really 'caught up' in it. He just happened to discover Jonas's body. He called the police right after that."

"Right," said Grayson, a frown puckering between his brows. He looked as if there might be more he wanted to say about that but instead he changed the subject. "Did Flora mention anyone being upset with her brother?"

I said, "Even though she and Jonas weren't close, she knew a couple of people who might have borne a grudge against him. His next-door neighbor was one of them. I know him from the library . . . his name's Reggie." I chuckled. "His conflict with Jonas was more of a brouhaha. I bet it didn't even register with Jonas that Reggie was unhappy with him. Jonas's dog's barking was driving Reggie nuts and he was displeased with a tree that fell from Jonas's yard into his yard, knocking down one of Reggie's fence panels."

Grayson raised his eyebrows as he pulled the car into my driveway. "That would definitely be aggravating."

"Yes, but enough to kill over? It seems really unlikely. And Reggie is this nerdy academic type. It's tough to picture him being involved."

"You said there were two people Flora mentioned?" asked Grayson.

"There was also Augusta Weber. She was apparently dating Jonas and he might have unceremoniously dumped her recently?"

"Do you think she might have wanted to murder Jonas for dumping her and dating someone else?" he asked.

"Well, William Congreve made the point that hell hath no fury like a woman scorned," I said.

Grayson looked thoughtful. "And this is why I go out with a librarian—to learn little tidbits. I thought Shakespeare came up with that phrase."

"It's been falsely attributed to him. And the direct quote from Congreve's play is somewhat different from my paraphrase." I gave Grayson a wry look. "And somehow, so many of my conversations abruptly turn back to literature. I should let you go—I know you've probably got to get over to the newspaper office."

He gave me a quick kiss which turned into a longer one. "See you tomorrow?" he asked, a bit hoarsely. I smiled at him and nodded.

The next day started off much quieter than the one before. I headed off to the library since I was the one scheduled to open up. Mornings, before anyone else got to the library, were my favorite time of day there. I got Fitz settled in (he'd happily trotted off to a favorite sunbeam he knew of), and then wandered around turning on the lights and watering the houseplants that were scattered around the library and in our breakroom.

Wilson came in precisely five minutes later and was wearing what I thought of as his "full armor—" a suit and tie and perfectly polished dress shoes. I lifted a hand to wave to him across the library and he gave a wave back, quickly heading to his office.

I hesitated for a moment before following him. I had the feeling that Wilson was still embarrassed over whatever his involvement in Jonas's death was. I wanted to make sure he realized that nothing had changed in our professional relationship.

"How are you holding up?" I asked.

He sighed. "I didn't sleep much last night."

The dark circles under his eyes attested to that.

I knew Wilson had insisted he wanted to get back to the library, but I said, "Are you sure you shouldn't be spending today at home? You could catch up on your sleep."

He shook his head and picked up one of the files on his desk, opening it and looking down. "No, thank you. Like I said, working is more of a distraction for me."

It was definitely a dismissal. I walked back out of his office and into the tech area to power up our computers there before patrons started arriving.

A few minutes later, Luna arrived, her face matching her hair—bright pink. She glanced around the library anxiously, then spotted me coming out of the tech area and hurried over.

"Where's Wilson?" she asked in a rush.

I nodded over to his office and we looked over to see Wilson completely engrossed in his file.

Luna blew out a sigh of relief. "Thank goodness. I was sure he was going to catch me for being late this time. And I've been so punctual lately! He never seems to catch me being on time—only when I've overslept or am running late."

She looked over at Wilson again, but he'd apparently lost focus and was staring blankly out of the glass windows of his office. "What's wrong with him?"

I'd promised Wilson I wouldn't say anything, so I said simply, "Wilson didn't get any sleep last night."

Luna made a face. "That's not good. He'd texted me and my mom this morning saying that he needed to speak with us today. It put both of us in a tizzy, especially since we hadn't been in touch with him yesterday. I thought I must be getting in trouble for something at work, but it didn't make sense that he wanted Mom to be here, too. And Mom thought maybe he wanted to break up with her, but that *also* didn't make any sense. So we started mulling over the possibilities and that's how I ended up running so late. Do you know what it's about?"

I quickly shook my head. Again, I had no intention of spilling Wilson's secrets. I had a feeling this impromptu meeting was when he was planning on telling both of them that he was involved in a police investigation. Burton had clearly not filled Luna in. But then, he was busy with the investigation. There might not have been time yesterday to get in touch with his girlfriend.

Luna sighed again. "Well, I guess we'll just find out later. I'm going to pick Mom up around lunchtime and bring her over here. I hope his meeting isn't anything that's going to upset our stomachs. Mom and I were planning on eating our lunches in the breakroom." She held up two insulated lunchboxes.

I was ready to get the focus off of Wilson and his assorted oddities that day. "How are things going with your book club? Is it still okay if I sit in on it for a while? I love the book."

Luna's face brightened. "Don't you love *The Westing Game*? It's one of my favorites."

"Mine too. I was glad for the opportunity to re-read it. I want to see what teenagers today make of it."

Luna grinned at her. "We'll find out! I hope they're going to like it just as much as we did."

And they did. Later that day, Luna hosted the club meeting. Attendance from teens had dramatically increased since Luna started working at the library. They seemed to find her really approachable. As they came in, they gave her hugs and high-fives. Luna asked them about what was going on in their lives—and they were *telling* her. It was a real gift—one that the parents of the teens likely wished they had. Luna had put snacks and drinks out and it was almost more of a party vibe than a club meeting. They talked about the book and the characters, what they'd *thought* was going to happen and how the book had surprised them. Luna did a fabulous job steering the topics and they all gave a round of applause at the end of the meeting. She gave a mock bow and laughed.

I helped Luna put the chairs away at the end of the meeting and she said in a low voice, "Hey, Wilson spoke with Mom and me."

"How did that go?"

Luna's eyes were big. "I mean, it went fine, but he didn't really tell us what was going on."

My heart sank a little bit. I could see Wilson not opening up to me but the fact he was keeping Mona, especially, in the dark wasn't good.

"All he said was that he was out running 'a personal errand' yesterday and ended up discovering Jonas Merchant's body." Luna shrugged. "It was like he was dropping a bomb and defusing it simultaneously. Mom was asking him if he knew Jonas and saying how upsetting it must have been and he really didn't engage with her at all. Do you know anything else about what happened?"

I shook my head. "Not really. Wilson called me yesterday morning and asked if I could drive him home from Jonas's house. He was just feeling a little shaky after finding his body."

"Well, of course he was! I can't imagine." But Luna looked a bit queasy, as if she could. "I'm surprised Burton didn't mention anything to me about it."

Luna and the police chief had been dating for months. They're sort of an odd couple with Luna the extraverted free spirit and Burton the quiet, cautious type.

"He's probably slammed with work right now. You know how things are when he's busy with a case."

Luna nodded. "It's aggravating, though. Wilson didn't go into any detail with me, either. Whatever his business was over at Jonas's house, it's pretty clear he wants to keep it private. Well, I hope it all blows over soon. Mom was trying to give him a hug and Wilson just looked really stiff and tense."

Luna changed the subject to library-related stuff then and we chatted for a few minutes as we finished tidying up the community room. Then I headed over to the circulation desk. It ended up being the kind of day where everything happened at once. And the kind of day where I didn't get accomplished what I'd originally planned. Instead, the copier went on the blink, two people needed help (at the same time) in the technology area, a student needed assistance finding resources for a paper she was writing, and a lady came over and spent a good deal of time talking to me for no real reason at all.

I left at five feeling pretty drained, unusual for a day at the library. Which was precisely when Grayson called me.

"Hey there," he said in that upbeat voice. "You're off now, right? I'm not interrupting anything?"

"Not a bit," I said, trying to match his peppiness but failing utterly. What I said was the truth, though. I was, at that moment, lying on my sofa with Fitz and a bowl of microwaved popcorn. I was hardly engaged in anything important.

"I know this is sort of last minute," he said, "But would you be interested in going to a concert with me tonight? One of our reporters had a couple of tickets and can't go, so I bought them off of him."

Grayson told me the name of the group, which was actually a group I liked listening to. But considering the fact that I was a blob on the sofa, I didn't think I had it in me to haul myself up, get dressed again (I was in yoga pants and an ancient tee shirt), and head out for a late night of music.

I made a face. Unfortunately, I'd also turned Grayson down for a couple of other things in the last couple of weeks. More fortunately, he was an understanding kind of guy.

"Hey, I'm really sorry," I said slowly. "I got slammed at work today and I haven't been able to peel myself off the sofa since I came home. Do you mind if I don't make it?"

Grayson said, "Of course not. I totally understand. Sorry you had such a crazy day at the library. I know it gets chaotic there sometimes."

"Yeah, just a bunch of really unexpected stuff that all seemed to happen at one time. You'd think a library would be a more peaceful place. But you should totally go. It's such a great band."

Grayson said, "It *is* a good band. I'm not sure I want to go by myself, though. Maybe I should just have an early night, myself."

This made me feel a bit guilty. Grayson dearly loved music and had introduced me to some great stuff. It was the main way that *he* relaxed, as opposed to my way—basically withdrawing from society with a book and a cat. But I didn't feel guilty enough to go to the concert.

"How about if you take someone else? You've got the extra ticket, after all. There's got to be someone who wants to go out tonight."

Grayson was quiet on the other end as he considered this for a few moments. "Well, there's Abby at work. She's crazy about music and goes to concerts all the time."

Boy, I'd really set myself up for that one. But I couldn't be ungracious enough to tell him he couldn't take another woman to a concert. "You should ask her if she wants to go," I said bravely.

He hesitated. "Are you sure that's okay with you?"

"Of course it is. There's no reason you shouldn't have a fun evening and enjoy a band just because I'm too pooped to go out. Tell Abby hi for me."

And tell her, I added silently, not to make any moves on you.

Chapter Five

The next day was more of a regular day at the library. That meant that there was still the element of the unexpected (broken equipment, computer questions, research help, a clogged-up toilet in the restroom), but it didn't happen all at once.

I was locking up the library that night so when five o'clock rolled around, I was still around when Hattie Gray walked in. She was a tall woman in her early fifties who had a fondness for tailored clothes. Hattie definitely qualified as a regular patron at the library—you could practically set a clock by her. As the high school principal, she liked to take work here to knock out before she headed home. I'd always thought that was a remarkably good way to separate office and home life while still being able to get out of the school and to a different environment to get work done. It was like she'd set up her own transition from work to home.

Usually, Hattie would speak a few words to me, then head over to the quiet section of the library with her laptop. Before she left, she'd come by the desk again to either check out a novel or nonfiction book and chat for a couple of minutes. She was a perpetual learner, even in her role as administrator. A true academic. Today, though, she came right over to the reference desk where I was working and looked like she wanted to talk. Considering Flora had mentioned to me that a neighbor had reported Hattie had recently been in touch with Jonas, I didn't mind speaking with her, either.

She smiled at me, but her smile was tight and tense. "Hi Ann," she said in a quiet voice.

"Hi Hattie," I said. "Is there anything I can help you with today?"

"Some information," she said. Then she gave a short laugh. "But not the kind of information I'm usually looking for. This would be more like . . . gossip."

"Well, I'll do my best," I said.

"I heard that Jonas Merchant died." Her voice was crisp.

I nodded. "That's correct."

"I also heard that you were at his house earlier when the police were there. I was wondering if you heard anything about his cause of death or any other pertinent information regarding him."

Hattie's delivery was all business, but I could see that there were a lot of conflicting emotions trying to break through the surface. It must be taking a lot of energy to suppress them.

"I was there, yes. I'm not sure how much I know about what happened, though," I said slowly. "I do know that the police are treating it as a homicide."

"He's definitely deceased then." Still that crisp voice.

I nodded. "That's correct."

Hattie's shoulders relaxed a little. "I see. So someone murdered him." She shook her head. "That's hardly a surprise, though, considering his behavior."

"His behavior?" I played dumb to hear what she'd say next.

"That's right. Jonas was not a good guy." Hattie was someone who always seemed to keep her emotions on lockdown. She gave a short laugh. "I'm not the only one who thought so. Of course, I didn't have anything to do with his death, but I'm not exactly sorry to have it confirmed."

I hesitated. So far, the consensus had been that Jonas was not "a good guy." But people had been remarkably cagey about why he was so terrible. The only definitely information so far was that he might have abruptly broken off a relationship with Augusta Weber and that he'd been a bad neighbor to Reggie Bartlett. But Ted and Hattie weren't exactly being forthcoming as to why they disliked Jonas so much . . . or why they thought everyone else did. "You knew him then?"

"Distantly." After a moment Hattie added, "Did the police seem to have any leads? I'm guessing you spoke with them, right?"

"If they did, they didn't share that information with me. Sorry." I decided not to mention that I knew Hattie herself was someone the police were inquiring about in connection to Jonas.

Hattie nodded stiffly and gave me a small smile. "Got it. I guess that makes sense—they're probably trying to keep information they discover quiet. Could you let me know if you *do* hear anything?"

I nodded and she relaxed a little bit. "Thanks, Ann. Well, I better get to work . . . I have a lot to knock out this evening. See you in a bit."

I watched her thoughtfully as she walked away. Hattie always seemed so tightly controlled that it was hard to picture her in any way connected to Jonas. But then, Wilson fit the same bill.

I glanced over at Wilson's office and saw him looking at the papers in front of him with a blank expression. Looking back over at Hattie, now settled at a table with her laptop, I saw much the same expression there.

The next few days went by quickly but without much stress. The pace at the library was steady, which was perfect for working on things like the library newsletter while still being able to help patrons and run one of the tech drop-ins. Grayson persuaded me to see a superhero movie with him one night after work and I found myself enjoying it a little more than I expected.

"See?" he said teasingly. "Next thing you know, I'll make you a fan of the Star Wars movies."

"That's going to take some doing," I said with a wry smile. "Somehow, I've just never been able to really get into them. But now, I have a request for *you*."

"Uh-oh," he said, making a face. "What's that?"

"How about if you come to film club at the library tomorrow? I know you usually can't make it because of work, but what good is being the editor of the newspaper if you can't be flexible?"

He chuckled. "Right you are. And I guess it's only fair for me to see something a little more highbrow considering I've managed to get you to see a Marvel movie. I'm scared to ask what's airing tomorrow—something with subtitles? A costume drama?"

I put my hands on my hips and gave him a mock scowl. "Is that all you think our film club watches? No wonder you haven't been able to make it. We do watch some foreign films, but we also watch a lot of really interesting classics that members of our group propose. Our club members are very diverse, too, in gender, age, and interests. And I think I'll keep the title of the movie a secret so it will be a surprise. I think you'll enjoy it—and all of our crew over there."

Now Grayson looked genuinely interested. "I'll look forward to it then."

That next day, I was pleased to see that Grayson was enjoying himself. I wasn't sure why I'd doubted that he would—he was one of those people who seemed to find something pleasurable in every situation he found himself in. He also managed to find common ground between himself and any random person he came across. Grayson immediately struck up a conversation with George, who owned the typewriter repair shop on the square. I figured that a newspaperman and a typewriter guy would probably have plenty to talk about and they did.

"I'll have to come by and take a look at your shop," Grayson was saying to him.

George chuckled. "It's a tiny little place on the square. Not much of a shop—more of a hole in the wall. And there's not a lot of room in there, so you might have to squeeze yourself in. It's jam-packed full of typewriters. Manual, electric, you name it."

"And you get that much business from people here locally? Or are customers shipping you typewriters and doing business with you online?"

"Mostly I've got online business. I do repairs, sell typewriters, sell typewriter parts . . . all of that stuff. My dad started the business back in the 70s and when he retired, I took over."

Grayson said, "He must have been proud that you did."

George snorted. "Not a bit. He told me I was crazy to take it on—by then, he could see the writing on the wall when it came to computers. He wanted me to leave Whitby and be a lawyer or an engineer or something. But I guess I had the typewriter bug by then. There were some lean years, but as soon as I went online, I found a niche market. The best part was that Dad was so excited that I was able to keep up the business."

George, who was usually a brash, crusty kind of guy, actually had a little moisture welling in his eyes.

Grayson was always one to know a good story when he saw one. "That's awesome, George. Would you be at all interested in being interviewed for the paper? I'm doing a recurring column profiling different people from around town and I'd love to do a feature."

George looked pleased and turned very slightly pink, which was sort of cute on the big, brusque man. "Sure. That would be great."

It had actually been George's turn to pick the film and so I finally had to rein in their conversation.

"Sorry to interrupt, but I think it's time for us to start. Do you want to give an intro?"

George glanced at the clock on the wall and said, "Sure thing! Sorry, I lost track of time there."

Grayson grinned, "I've been told I'll enjoy the movie today. Are you the one who chose it?"

"I did and you're in for a treat, man. We're watching *The Maltese Falcon*, one of the best noir films around. Seen it before?"

Grayson shook his head. "I've been kind of in a rut in terms of what I've been watching. Ann is trying to get me out of it. Honestly, unless they're Christmas movies, I haven't seen a lot of classic films at all."

"A little Humphrey Bogart will fix that," said George. "These films are classics for a reason, man."

We all sat down as George gave an enthusiastic introduction for the 1941 film. He also plugged the Dashiell Hammett novel it was based on. I hurried out of the room to grab the couple of copies from the stacks in case anyone wanted to check them out after the movie was over. Then I sat next to Grayson and we munched on the popcorn I'd brought in as we watched Sam Spade work his magic.

When the film wrapped up, there was a round of applause and a few whistles.

"Did you like it?" I asked, although I already knew the answer. I'd watched Grayson's rapt attention as the movie played.

"Loved it," he said with a grin. "I think you might have made a classic film convert."

"The university plays classic films every month, too—we'll have to check it out next time," I said, grinning back at him.

After George and I led the group in a discussion about the film (Mona was there and was apparently a tremendous Bogart fan), Grayson helped me clean up the community room and put the chairs away.

We were talking about movies we'd enjoyed in the past and Grayson was thinking about which one might be good for the film club when there was a light tap at the open door. A blonde woman in her early thirties was there grinning at Grayson. She seemed restless and full of life and only had eyes for Grayson. She wore what looked like expensive clothes and had the sort of makeup that made it look as if she weren't wearing makeup at all.

"Hi there," she said. "I thought I recognized your car out front. I ran by to find some photos in the Whitby historical archive."

"Got it!" said Grayson with a return grin. He turned to me and said, "Ann, I don't think you've met Abby."

Chapter Six

Ah. Abby, the coworker who went to the concert with Grayson the other night when I was too wiped to go. I tried to change my rather plastic smile to a genuine one, which I felt I was able to do with some difficulty. "Great to meet you, Abby."

Abby reluctantly tore her gaze away from Grayson. "Likewise. Thanks for sharing Grayson with me. For the concert, I mean. That was such a great group. I added so much music to my playlist after seeing them."

This opened up a whole other line of conversation where the two of them talked about playlists and the difficulty of discovering new music when algorithms were suggesting things that were similar to what you were already listening to. I continued clearing up the room and tried to look like I wasn't feeling a bit concerned about Abby, who seemed smart, witty, and lovely.

"Well," Abby finally said breezily, "I should head back to the archive room. I didn't realize you worked here, Ann."

Grayson looked at me fondly. "Ann practically runs the place."

I gave a tight smile, "No, that would be Wilson. I'm just second in command and that's mostly because I've been here forever."

"I'm sure the library has got to be an interesting place to work," said Abby. Her voice was loaded with doubt. She gave us a cheery wave as she headed to the back of the library.

"I suppose I should be heading back to work, myself," said Grayson ruefully. "Thanks for the break, though—great film. Oh, there was one other thing I wanted to ask you. You're off tomorrow, right?"

I nodded and Grayson said, "I think I'm going to attend Jonas Merchant's funeral service. Not because I knew him, of course, but just to be there to cover it as a reporter in case I find out anything. Would you like to come with me?"

"Sure. I don't have any plans for tomorrow." Attending a funeral was hardly a date, but seeing how eager Abby was to see Grayson, I figured it wouldn't hurt to spend a little extra time with my boyfriend.

"Great." He smiled at me. "I'll pick you up about 10:45. Then maybe we can grab supper out tomorrow night."

Seeing his smile warmed me up inside and any possible threat Abby represented quickly disappeared in my mind.

The next day was a gloomy one, which definitely set the stage for the funeral. Flora had planned a graveside service. Jonas was apparently not a church-going man, but Flora had her minister at the graveside. The cemetery was the only one in town and the gravestones ranged from practically ancient to just weeks old. A canopy of trees stretched over the plot. Flora gave me a smile when she spotted me. There weren't many people at the service, so I was glad I was there, no matter the reason. I suspected the folks who *were* there were friends of Flora and were just there to support her.

The minister read some verses and we recited the Lord's prayer. Then he spoke for a few minutes before Flora stood and nervously walked over to join him and to address the group. She cleared her throat. "Thank you all for being here for me today. And to be here for Jonas, too. I know he wasn't the very best man he could be. But he was a good brother to me when we were young. I do have some happy memories of the two of us and I'm thankful for that."

Flora paused for a moment as if trying to think of anything else to say about Jonas. Then she gave an apologetic smile, thanked us again, and hurried back to her seat.

I thought it was pretty terrible if someone had to look decades back in time in order to find something good to say about you at your own funeral. Flora's tribute had been generous and she had given him a nice send-off.

I noticed Augusta Weber was in attendance. I figured Grayson didn't know who she was so I quietly filled him in. He glanced her way with interest. Augusta was a wiry woman with strawberry-blonde hair and a smattering of light freckles on her face. She noticed me looking in her direction and gave me a small smile. Considering the fact that Jonas had apparently rather precipitously ended their relationship, I thought it was generous for her to be there.

I spotted Ted Hill there, too, which surprised me. He certainly hadn't seemed to be a fan of Jonas's when we were at his garage. Ted was watching the proceedings with a grim expression on his face. Perhaps he was there simply to ensure Jonas was truly gone.

Reggie Bartlett, Jonas's neighbor, was in attendance, as well. I raised my eyebrows a little. It was quite the collection of people who hadn't been very fond of Jonas or who had some sort of issue with him. I saw Reggie's attention was completely focused on Flora, so that might explain why he was there.

The service quickly wrapped up and Flora stood with the minister to receive condolences. Grayson and I both spoke with her and she looked grateful that we were there. There were lines of stress around her mouth and eyes and she looked as if she hadn't been getting much sleep.

Grayson and I were walking slowly back to our cars when Augusta caught up with us. "Hi Ann."

She looked curiously at Grayson and I quickly said, "Good to see you, Augusta. This is Grayson Phillips, a friend of mine."

They shook hands and then Augusta said, "How is everything going at the library? I haven't been able to make it over there for a while. I need to get back and find something to read. I haven't been able to fall asleep at night and I have a feeling it has to do with not having a book to read before I turn in."

"Oh, everything has been good over there . . . it's been really busy, which is nice. Our construction is all done, if you haven't been by for a while. You'll be amazed how great it all looks. I'd be happy to help you find a couple of books to check out, too. You're a fan of Jodi Picoult, aren't you?"

Augusta gave Grayson a wry look. "Can you believe she can remember these kinds of details? I can't even remember what I did yesterday." She turned back to me. "Yes, I love her books."

"She's got a new book out that I think you'll really enjoy. It'll be a quick read, so you might want to check out more than one book so you'll have something to read after you're done with it."

Augusta said, "Great! I'll be sure to run by there soon. It's been on my list for ages to get over there." She paused. "On a totally different topic, I was just curious—how did you two know Jonas?"

"We didn't, really. But we wanted to come to show our support for Flora. I've known her for years from the library and I spend a lot of time over at the garden center, too. She's become a friend of mine."

"Oh, that makes sense. Flora probably checks out a lot of books about horticulture, doesn't she?" said Augusta. "I wish I knew her a little better."

Grayson asked politely, "So you were more of a friend of Jonas?"

Augusta gave a crooked smile. "As well as anyone could really know Jonas. He wasn't the easiest nut to crack, even though I dated him for a while. He never really wanted to spend much time with Flora, so I didn't see her very often. Whenever she *did* go by his house, he was pretty curt with her and she left shortly after she arrived. He was fairly . . . disinterested in his family. I thought at first it might have something to do with Flora herself, but she seems lovely. It was just Jonas. Now I realize he caused most of the issues he was dealing with."

I said carefully, "Sometimes it's hard to really get to know a person until you've been around them for a while."

"Especially if that person happens to be Jonas Merchant." Augusta gave a short laugh. "He kept to himself in many ways but he seemed to know everything about everybody."

"Did the two of you date long?" I couldn't really imagine the two of them together. Maybe Jonas had done a good job hiding his true nature while they were dating.

"About six months. Then, out of nowhere, Jonas ended the relationship." Augusta shrugged. "I was completely caught off-guard. Everything seemed to be going fine. We were in a routine together. The bad thing is that I figured out later that I was actually the last person to know about the end of our relationship."

I winced. "Oh no."

"Yeah. He was dating somebody else and friends of mine had seen them out together—right out in public like he didn't even care. They let me know about it right away. He wasn't even trying to conceal the fact that he was seeing someone else. Can you believe it?"

From what I'd heard about Jonas, I could definitely believe it. He didn't strike me as the kind of person who put a lot of thought into other people's feelings.

"Anyway, obviously I wanted to confront him with it after I found out. He didn't answer my phone calls. So I went over to his house and he didn't answer his door. Finally, I heard from him. He'd broken up with me by *text*. Not the most adult way to end things."

And it was a cowardly method I'd heard employed by someone else I knew some time ago. It was an approach that hadn't gone well.

Grayson asked, "Did Jonas apologize? Or give any kind of explanation as to why he was ending the relationship?"

Augusta snorted. "You clearly didn't know Jonas."

Grayson shook his head.

"He wouldn't even answer my phone calls. He couldn't even be an adult enough to pick up the phone and talk to me about how he'd cheated on me—how he'd *humiliated* me in public. Everyone in town knew we were a couple. I was so hurt and angry at his behavior."

"Of course you were," I said. "That was incredibly disrespectful and hurtful of him."

Augusta shrugged. "Eventually, I had to just let it go. He wasn't going to talk to me and there was nothing I could do. I just drowned my sorrows for a few days. My friends convinced me that I'd had a lucky escape."

"Very true," I said.

Grayson asked, "When did this all happen?"

"That's the thing—it was less than two weeks ago. So of course someone told the cops about how upset I was with Jonas and they've been talking to me like I'm some sort of suspect in his death. And I don't even have a real alibi. I was at work, came home, read for a while, then went to bed. Got up, went to work. No one was there to verify where I was because I had no idea I *needed* an alibi. Jonas seemed like the kind of guy who was going to live forever."

Grayson asked, "Do you know who the other woman is? Is she here at the funeral service?"

"I know who she is. But she's not here today. I'm kind of surprised. Maybe they weren't that much of an item yet. Or maybe she'd realized the kind of guy he was and decided to end the relationship before it really went anywhere."

Or maybe the other woman didn't want to be considered a suspect by showing up, I thought. Burton was in attendance at the funeral and was certainly keeping an eye on everyone. He was watching us talk to Augusta with interest.

"It was nice of you to come to the funeral, considering what happened between you two," said Grayson.

Augusta gave a small shrug. "I usually try to take the high ground. Besides, I wanted to give his sister my condolences."

She paused for a couple of moments and then said, "This whole thing has led to some soul searching on my behalf. I've had some revelations about my taste in men."

"You have?" I asked.

"Thinking back through the years, even when I was in high school with you, Ann, I never went for the wholesome type of guy. I always seemed to be attracted to the men who were going to be trouble or cause some sort of drama. Maybe now that I've figured this out, I can stop the pattern before it happens again."

"At least something good has come out of it, then," I said with a smile.

We glanced over the assembled group and the little pockets of people talking to each other. Then Grayson said, "Do you have any ideas about who might have done this to Jonas? You knew him pretty well."

Augusta sighed. "I wish I did. If I could redirect the cops away from me, it would be really helpful. It sure sounds like a lot of people were unhappy with Jonas. The only person I can think of is Flora." She looked at me. "Sorry, Ann. I know she's a friend of yours. And I feel really bad saying it because I didn't know her very well and I was just saying I wanted to give her my condolences. But Jonas would always tell me that Flora wanted a house with a yard because she enjoyed gardening. The thing was, I got the impression that Flora had taken care of their dad in the years before his death. She must have been really frustrated that Jonas ended up with the house. But who knows? I'm sure there were other people who must have been just as upset with Jonas as she was."

Including, unfortunately, Wilson.

Augusta glanced across the cemetery and then glanced at her watch. "Well, I should be getting along. Good seeing you, Ann. Nice meeting you, Grayson."

Grayson watched her thoughtfully as she headed away. "She didn't sound like someone who wanted to exact revenge because of being dumped."

"No. Besides, from everything I've heard about Jonas, it sounds as if she really had a lucky escape." I paused. "It looks like Ted Hill is heading this way."

Chapter Seven

Ted looked like he wanted to speak with us, too. I'd noticed while we were talking with Augusta that Ted had been speaking with Burton. I wondered if he'd thought of some information to share with him.

But before Ted reached us, there was a grim throat-clearing cough behind us that made me jump. It was Zelda Smith, our red-haired, chain-smoking homeowner association president. She'd finally succeeded in wrangling Grayson onto the HOA board and I felt sure she'd hadn't entirely given up on convincing me to join. She'd been trying to persuade me for years and I'd told her the library didn't give me much free time. Which was true, but even more true was the fact that I didn't want the little free time I had to go to an HOA board. Sadly, I was providing Zelda with lots of time to try and convince me otherwise because she'd started volunteering at the library several times a week.

Grayson was always a lot more encouraging to Zelda than I was. He smiled at her and said, "Well, hi there! How's my favorite neighbor?"

Zelda preened a bit at this even though she was too hard-boiled to really believe his flattery. "Good. Well, fair, I guess. I'm at a funeral, after all."

"Did you know Jonas?" I asked curiously. It didn't seem to me that Jonas's path would cross with Zelda's often.

"I certainly did," said Zelda crisply. "I had to speak to him *several* times on behalf of the HOA about the state of his yard. Young Reggie Bartlett tried to get me to intervene for him about a fence issue, as well."

"It's generous of you to come out to his service, then. Considering he'd been something of an issue in the neighborhood," I said.

Zelda sniffed. "Despite the problems he caused, it was important to have the neighborhood represented at his funeral. I also wanted to support Flora, who I *do* know well. She's helped with the landscaping at the entrance to the subdivision. And, of course, I'm thrilled Flora is going to be moving into the house and sprucing things up." She turned to Grayson and said, "Do you think you could take a look at that architectural review request after you return from the service?"

Grayson said, "I wish I could, but I've got to grab lunch and get back to the newspaper office. Tell you what, though—I'll get to it just as soon as I get home tonight."

Zelda frowned at this. "I suppose that will have to do. I'm rather busy, myself, since I'm on my way to the library."

I stifled a sigh. On the one hand, Zelda was frightfully efficient when she was at the library and got tons of shelving done as well as any other task we threw her way. On the other, she felt like a sort of malevolent presence there—giving discouraging looks to patrons needing help and glowering at people who were idly chatting with each other. It was a double-edged sword.

My feelings must have been fairly evident because Grayson's eyes crinkled at me in amusement.

"Are you going to be at the library today, Ann?" asked Zelda. She looked as if she might disapprove of the idea of my not being there.

"I sure will. I have a late shift today and will be there right after lunch."

Zelda seemed to accept this answer. She bobbed her head and said, "See you later, then." Then she stomped off to her car.

"Is it me, or does she always seem to be in a bad mood?" I asked. "Let's wait a second before we head over to the cars so we won't accidentally catch up with her."

Grayson said mildly, "Oh, she just *seems* grim. I'm sure she has a lighter side to her."

I wasn't at all sure this was the case. As soon as she had gotten a safe distance ahead, we walked to Grayson's car and headed off to lunch.

We were eating sandwiches outside at the deli near the library when Grayson said, "Hey, since it's been kind of an unsettling day, how about if we go out tonight? Some friends of mine invited me over for supper and they were interested in meeting you."

Whenever I heard any sort of invitation to do anything, especially if it was on the spur of the moment, I immediately felt a tremendous urge to turn it down. The introvert in me never wanted to do anything but curl up at night with a book and the cat. Fortunately, I had an excellent excuse and one that Grayson had apparently forgotten about.

"Actually, I've got the late shift—I'll be heading out at nine instead of five." I tried to sound sorry about this.

Grayson said, "Oh, I totally forgot that. I guess in my head I was thinking you'd be leaving the library at five. Ugh. Okay, maybe next time."

He looked disappointed and I felt a little guilty about letting him down. I knew there was no way I could have made it because of work, but it was the fact that I was glad I wasn't going out that made me feel worse. The fact of the matter was that Grayson was a lot more outgoing than I was.

I reached out and gave his hand a squeeze. "Sorry. Hope you have fun with your friends tonight. Who's going to be there?"

He brightened and regaled me with a list of his friends. I'd met one of them briefly when we'd been out at a restaurant. They all sounded like good guys. "The guys know Abby, too, because she used to work with Jeremy before she got into journalism. Jeremy said she might stop by."

The ubiquitous Abby. I was still curious about Grayson's coworker, especially considering the amount of time it seemed like they were spending together. I said brightly, "Well, that should be fun."

Grayson seemed oblivious to how fake my voice sounded to my own ears. "Hope she can make it. And Peter, too, of course."

"Peter?"

"Her fiancé. Haven't you met him? I thought I'd introduced him when we were eating lunch that day."

I said, "Oh . . . *that's* who Peter was. I remember you saying he was dating someone you worked with."

"Abby, yes. Anyway, we'll find a time for you to really properly meet everybody."

I felt a surprising amount of relief at this revelation. I knew I'd been bothered by Abby, but I guess it hadn't really sunk in just how much I had been. "Hey, I really appreciate your patience with me and my crazy schedule."

Grayson looked confused as if he somehow hadn't realized I'd been difficult to schedule with. Or that, perhaps, I'd deliberately dragged my heels sometimes just because I hadn't wanted to go out. "I just treasure the time we *do* spend together, Ann. I know we're both busy, and I know you and I have some different interests. But that's part of the reason this works."

I reached across and held his hand tightly again, enjoying the sun and being with him.

We finished up our lunch and then Grayson dropped me off at the house so I could drive to the library. I collected Fitz and we headed out to work.

Zelda, as promised, was already there and grimly shelving books. I'd found that Zelda was something of a shelving machine. She would get into a zone and then wouldn't want to be interrupted. Naturally, that's exactly when patrons would interrupt her to ask her where the books on hold were or how to find a particular novel they were looking for. Zelda didn't like being interrupted from her shelving and would give the patrons very aggrieved looks. But she rarely sent them my way. As little as she liked being interrupted, she liked *me* to be interrupted even less. She'd bark at them if they tried to approach me.

Wilson was sitting in his office and looked inquiringly at me when he saw me coming in so I walked over. "How did things go at the service?" he asked quietly.

"Flora had a good group of people there to support her," I said. "It all went really well. I'm sure she's relieved that it's over, though."

"Did you have a chance to speak with anyone there? Have you been able to find out any information related to Jonas's death?" His voice was low even though no one would be able to hear us unless we were shouting.

I nodded. "The general consensus is that many people disliked Jonas for various reasons. He wasn't the most popular person in town. The police seem to be speaking with several people, at least. I don't think you're the main suspect, Wilson."

He relaxed his shoulders a little and gave me a nod back. "That's a relief to hear," he said gruffly. "He did seem to go out of his way to make trouble for other people."

I said, "I hope you've been able to plan something to get your mind off all of this. Maybe going out to dinner with Mona? A distraction could be the best thing for you."

I saw his eyes shutter and he immediately shook his head, looking tense again. "Not right now, I think. Let's let the dust settle. I don't want to involve Mona in any of this mess. Maybe Burton will arrest someone soon and things will be different."

Apparently, he was still concerned he was a primary suspect in Jonas's death. Was he punishing himself by not enjoying himself? Or was he just wanting to spare Mona association with a suspect in a murder investigation, as he mentioned? Either way, I had the feeling he wasn't communicating with Mona about his motives. She was probably left wondering why he was isolating himself like he was.

I walked back out to the library and saw Luna walking over from the children's section with a quizzical look on her face.

"Is he talking?" she asked, her brow puckering.

"Sort of, but not really. He wanted to hear how Jonas's service was. He let me do most of the talking. And he shut me down when I suggested he have a break and take your mom out to dinner."

Luna rolled her eyes. "Okay, well, he's driving my mother crazy. She doesn't have much else to do so she's spending her time worrying about Wilson. He's been really brusque on the phone and hasn't made any overtures to her at all."

I said, "She knows he's just brushing her off because of his involvement with the case, right? I hope she's not taking it personally."

"It's sort of hard *not* to take it personally, but I think she's keeping it in perspective. Mom's a little hurt by his behavior, but mostly just worried about him. I'm glad it's not the other way around. Mom has been trying to get him to do things with her—inviting him to watch a movie at her house and stuff like that. But he's been pretty brusque with her." She chuckled. "I was thinking about setting up an 'accidental' meeting between them, sort of like *The Parent Trap*."

"Yeah, but the only problem with that is that Wilson is in such a sour mood right now that Mona wouldn't have any fun, much less Wilson. Which sort of defeats the purpose. Maybe things will be better after a little time goes by."

Luna sidled up a bit closer and asked, "Any information that you've been able to find out? I mean, Burton does a great job as a cop, but let's face it—people tend to freeze up and go silent when a police officer is asking them questions."

"I have found out a few things and actually, I need to get in touch with Burton to fill him in. Are you planning on seeing him today?"

Sometimes Burton would come by and take Luna to lunch, although lunchtime was definitely over now.

Luna shook her head. "Not today. At least, nothing is planned for today. But then, most of his time right now is taken up with the murder. You might want to go ahead and give him a call. But please go ahead and give me a preview. What have you found out?"

I said, "Well, I've mostly found out that Jonas wasn't a very popular guy, but you might have already guessed that."

"Flora will apparently get the house now, but I just can't picture her having anything to do with Jonas's death," I said staunchly.

"I know you can't. You're a great friend, Ann. And you're probably right—Flora has always seemed really gentle to me. But you know how sometimes with family there's a straw that breaks the camel's back. The house might have been that straw. I thought it was absolutely ridiculous that Jonas ended up with the house instead of Flora when their dad died. Flora was her dad's caretaker, for heaven's sake. Jonas completely washed his hands of helping out, moved away, and then *he* ended up with the house? Unbelievable."

I nodded. "Flora wants a place where she can do some gardening. She doesn't really have a yard right now so all of her gardening is just theoretical. I guess she'll have the house now, of course."

"Finally. She should have gotten it right away."

I added, "Then Burton and I chatted with Reggie Bartlett. So Burton was there with me for the first two conversations. Anyway, Reggie had a tough time with Jonas as a neighbor."

Luna rolled her eyes. "I can only imagine. I've driven by the house and the yard was always a real disaster. I mean, Mom is complaining that I haven't trimmed the bushes, but at least I cut the grass and try to make the yard look pretty decent. Was Reggie's issue with the yard?"

"Partly. He wasn't happy with the state of the property and there was also a fallen tree that Jonas didn't want to take care of that had ended up in Reggie's yard."

"Which shouldn't have been Reggie's problem," said Luna. "He comes into the library a lot, doesn't he?"

I nodded. "That's right. He teaches at the college. He doesn't really seem like the kind of guy who would flip out over a neighbor's yard issues and a barking dog, but I guess you never know Still, it seems like a silly reason to kill somebody."

"Poor dog," said Luna.

"I know. I tend to think that a dog that barks too much outside is being neglected. The good news is that Flora took the dog in. Bandit, I think his name was. I'm sure she's doting on him. She's such a nature and animal lover."

"Okay, so we have Flora who might have wanted Jonas's house and Reggie who might have wanted a different neighbor. Who else is there?"

"Ted Hill is a suspect." I was careful not to say anything about the murder weapon being an automotive tool since Burton had asked me to keep it to myself. "He seemed to really dislike Jonas, but I don't have any idea why he did. At any rate, the police seem interested in him."

Luna brightened. "That's intriguing. Anyone else?"

"There's Hattie Gray."

"What? The principal who's in here all the time after work?" Luna tilted her head to the side to consider this. "I can't see it."

"Apparently so. She asked me to confirm Jonas's death and a neighbor apparently reported that Hattie had been seen at Jonas's house. And then there's Augusta Weber, too."

Luna frowned. "That's a name I don't know."

"She comes in here, but she's pretty much in and out and wouldn't be in the children's section at all. Augusta was dating Jonas and then he ended things really abruptly. She didn't seem very happy about that." I shrugged.

"Nor should she have been. No one likes feeling like they've just been tossed aside." Luna looked suddenly cheerful. "Well, this is a fair-sized collection of suspects. I was worried that Wilson was going to be the only one and Mom would be dating a jailbird. Maybe Wilson will be able to return to normal life pretty soon. And start taking my mom out to dinner again," said Luna with a sigh.

At the mention of Wilson, we both looked over to his office right when he looked up from his work. He gave us a grumpy look and turned away.

"Guess we'd better get back to it," said Luna quickly. "Considering Wilson's current mood, I sure don't want to be on his bad side. Or Zelda's."

Zelda was bustling toward us with a metal cart stacked full of books and looked even grouchier than Wilson did. Luna hurried back to the children's department and I slid behind the reference desk to work on the library newsletter. One of the fun sections of our newsletter was an advice column called "Dear Fitz." Everyone from kids to seniors emailed us questions and "Fitz" would answer them. The questions ranged from what a normal day for Fitz looked like to questions with more of a research angle to them.

After writing the answer to this month's question (which was from an elementary-age patron who wanted to know why the sky was blue), I set about taking pictures around the library to illustrate the newsletter. For this, I'd need at least a couple of good pictures of Fitz, but I also liked to get some photos of the fireplace in the reading area, and the outside of the library itself (if the light cooperated). Grayson sometimes helped me out with photos since he had professional camera equipment, but I'd run out of the ones he'd provided and it was time for some fresh material for the newsletter.

Fitz was in the middle of a nap, but when he saw me, he gave a little trill and immediately posed himself in several fetching ways, rolling on his back, giving me a wry smile, playfully batting at a toy I dangled in front of him. I snapped off a ton of pictures, hoping several of them would be newsletter-worthy. Then I left him alone to curl back up into a ball and fall into a deep sleep, having done an amazing job, as usual.

I didn't get a chance to load the images into the newsletter right away because the reference desk became suddenly very busy. There was a woman trying to find a newspaper article about her grandmother from many decades ago, a teenager who needed some help finding resources for a paper he was writing, and a senior with some questions about using a new e-reader that he couldn't figure out how to load books on.

I'd just finished up helping with the e-reader when Burton strode into the library. I waved a hand in greeting, figuring he was just going to walk by and head over to the children's section to say hi to Luna while he was in the area. But he came right over to me instead, a grim look on his face.

"Everything okay?" I asked, suddenly getting the feeling that everything might not be.

Burton shook his head grimly. "I'm afraid not. We found Ted Hill dead a couple of hours ago."

Chapter Eight

My eyes opened wide. "You're kidding."

"Wish I was, but no. I found him, myself. I'd gone by with a deputy to have a talk with him again. He was, by far, our number one suspect, considering the murder weapon came from his shop and even had his fingerprints on it. When I got there, his door was unlocked and slightly ajar and he wasn't answering his doorbell. I walked right inside." Burton's face darkened at the memory.

"I'm so sorry. That must have been awful. I'm assuming he didn't die from natural causes?" Ted seemed pretty young to be suddenly struck down by a medical problem.

Burton shook his head. "It was blunt force trauma. I can't really divulge anything else but it sure wasn't an accident."

I nodded. "Got it. I'm sorry to hear that . . . Ted seemed like a good guy. I'm glad you've come in—I did want to talk to you about some things that I'd heard. And people I talked to."

Burton nodded, taking out the small notebook and pencil he kept in a pocket. "I was hoping you'd say that. Was one of the people Ted Hill, by any chance?"

"Yes. Although I didn't get as much information as I hoped I would. He struck me as a guy who liked to keep to himself. It was obvious he couldn't stand Jonas but didn't explain why. He was really close-lipped about the whole thing. Although I did get the feeling that he was holding something back at one point. That's not a lot of help to you, though."

Burton paused. "Have you spoken with Hattie Gray at all? I was thinking that I see her in here pretty regularly."

"That's right—she comes in here just about every day after school is over to do some work. I did speak to her about Jonas's death."

Burton said grimly, "The reason I ask is because Hattie was in a relationship with Ted. Did you know anything about that?"

This surprised me. Hattie was married and had been for a long while. Plus, I knew the hours she kept and wondered how she could even have fit in the time for an affair.

"But what business could that have been of Jonas's? I mean . . . I can understand how Hattie could possibly be connected to Ted's death if it was a matter of love-gone-wrong. How does that connect with Jonas, though?"

Then I said slowly, "Unless Jonas was blackmailing Hattie."

Burton looked relieved at the way I'd connected the dots without his having to connect them for me. "Bingo."

"If Jonas was a blackmailer, it explains why people weren't crazy about him," I continued. "I guess you found evidence of his activities when you searched his house?"

"That's right. He had a notebook where he kept track of payments and that kind of thing. He had quite a racket going on."

"Was Jonas blackmailing Ted, too?" I asked.

Burton shook his head. "No. But his sister was a victim of Jonas's. That needs to be kept between you and me," he added quickly.

I nodded soberly. "That's awful. So Ted actually had two people in his life being blackmailed by Jonas. No wonder you were on your way over to talk to him. He must have looked like the prime suspect. So, then, going back to Hattie. I didn't know what her connection to Jonas was, but now I'm assuming she was being blackmailed by him, as well? Do you know anything about that?"

Burton said, "Nothing I want to disclose right now. But your assumptions are correct. Did Hattie say anything to you about Jonas's death? Or about Jonas himself?"

"Not really, but Hattie is a pretty self-contained person. She likes to keep her emotions to herself. She was just speaking with me to confirm that Jonas was dead and to find out if I had any additional information. Which I didn't—at least, nothing I needed to share with Hattie."

Burton nodded. "Anybody else you've spoken with?"

"Augusta. I saw her at the funeral, of course."

Burton bobbed his head. "I remember seeing the two of you having a conversation."

"I didn't really find out anything especially earth-shattering from her. She was there to pay her respects to Flora, mainly. She and Jonas had been dating, which I'm sure you know. Until Jonas broke off the relationship, of course. It sounds like she was just chalking up the whole relationship to just a bad experience. It sounded like she was seeing a pattern in her dating life . . . one she wanted to stop."

"Anybody else?" asked Burton.

"That was it. Well, there were Flora and Reggie Bartlett, but you were there when they were talking about Jonas. I did speak with Flora another time at the nursery, but she just told me what you already know—that the police were asking her about Ted Hill and Hattie Gray."

Burton put his notebook away and said, "Thanks for this, Ann." He glanced across the library at Wilson. I'd noticed while talking to Burton that Wilson had been stealing glances at us. "How are things going with your director?"

"Wilson has been pretty upset by all this. He's just hoping you get a good lead to find out who killed Jonas . . . and now, I guess, Ted."

Burton said, "Has he been acting differently at all since this started?"

I hesitated. Wilson of course *had* been acting differently, but not because he seemed guilty. The last thing I wanted to do was make Wilson look bad. "He's been different, but only because he's so anxious about being caught up in this situation. He hasn't wanted to maintain his personal relationship because he doesn't want Mona to be involved in the investigation even tangentially."

I felt an uneasy sensation in my stomach thinking about Wilson. Could Jonas have been blackmailing him? What on earth could Wilson possibly have done to attract the attention of a blackmailer?

Burton said, "Where has Wilson been today?"

I answered promptly, "Here."

"The entire day?"

I said, "Absolutely. I can vouch for it. He's been in the building the whole day—he brought his lunch in and ate it in the breakroom. He's been keeping a very low profile."

"He couldn't have slipped out at some point this afternoon?" asked Burton.

"Not a chance. I've been at this desk all afternoon—he couldn't have gotten past me without my seeing. His car is in the back parking lot."

Burton nodded. "Sounds like he's got an excellent alibi, then." To his credit, he didn't sound regretful, even though it would mean wrapping up the case.

"Maybe this will help Wilson in terms of Jonas's death, too? If he didn't murder Ted, he shouldn't have been Jonas's murderer, either."

Burton said, "It doesn't hurt, that's for sure. Although it doesn't totally exonerate him from being a suspect in Jonas's death. Thanks for this, though, Ann."

He headed over to speak with Wilson, who was now looking even more uncomfortable than he had previously. Then, after Burton spent some time with him and apparently told him about Ted's death, he looked both grim and relieved at having an alibi.

The afternoon became much busier for me after that. I had a group of high school students who needed help finding resources for a project. Then someone needed help in our technology room with creating a spreadsheet.

By the time things got quieter there, Luna and Wilson had already clocked out for the day and it was seven-thirty. I never minded nights at the library, although I liked mornings there better. At night, though, there were often patrons who were working hard trying to complete whatever project or assignment they were working on. There were night owls who were reading or trying to find books to take home with them. And yes, there was the occasional patron that I'd have to wake up from a sound sleep, too. But it was very quiet.

When the doors opened, I glanced up from the desk where I was working on my library column. Hattie Gray was there and walking toward me with determination. Her face was lined with worry and she looked as though she'd been crying.

"Hi Hattie," I said slowly. "Is everything okay?" Everything clearly wasn't, but I wasn't sure what else to say.

"Hey," she said. She glanced around us to make sure we were alone. We were very much by ourselves with all of the patrons scattered in both the quiet study area and the periodicals section. "Can I talk to you for a few minutes?"

"Of course you can," I said, pushing my laptop to the side.

Hattie leaned across the desk a little and kept her voice low. "Do you know Ted Hill?"

"I do. Not very well, but I've been a customer of his for years at the auto shop." I hesitated. "I heard some sad news about him today."

Hattie drew back a little. "It's true, then?"

I nodded. "Yes. I heard it from an official source, I'm afraid. Were you a friend of Ted's?"

Hattie leaned again on the desk, but this time it looked as if she was looking for a bit of support from it. "Yes," she said. "I was. A parent called me on the phone to let me know what happened, but I wasn't sure it was true. Ted's son is a student at the school and this mom thought, as the principal, that I should be aware of what happened."

"His son wasn't at home, though, was he?" I asked with concern.

Hattie shook her head absently. "I don't think so. At least, that's what this parent said. Ted and his wife are separated and their son has spent the last couple of weeks with his mom. So, did this just happen then? This afternoon?"

"That's what I understand. I'm sorry that I don't have much information." I paused again, not really sure how to broach my question. Then I said, "Hattie, does this somehow connect with what we were talking about last time? About your dislike for Jonas and Jonas's death?"

Hattie didn't immediately answer. Then she took a deep breath. "You'll keep this quiet, won't you, Ann? I know we're not close friends or anything, but I really need someone to talk to right now. Honestly, it's easier to tell this to you than to someone I know well but who might be disappointed in me."

"Of course I will," I said. I knew it was a promise I could keep since it sounded like Burton already knew Hattie's secret.

Hattie nodded. "I'm not proud of it, but the fact is that Ted and I were having an affair. Ted is divorced, of course, but I'm still a married woman. What's more, as principal of the school, I'm expected to be a good role model for the kids. What makes it even worse is that Ted's son is a pupil at my school." She rubbed her forehead, looking drained. "Obviously, I didn't make a good decision."

"Everyone makes poor decisions from time to time," I said softly.

"The thing is that I still care for my husband. The last thing I want to do is hurt him. I never intended for him to find out about this affair. Now it looks like his finding out is practically inevitable. The police already know about Ted and me because of papers that Jonas had in his house. Jonas was trying to blackmail me, which they also know. Now that Ted's gone, they're going to be asking even more questions."

"And you're wanting to stay with your husband," I said.

"Absolutely. The affair between Ted and me was casual. Neither one of us was talking about us having a future together."

"Did the affair last long?" I asked.

Hattie sighed. "Longer than it should have. We'd been seeing each other for about six months. Not often because sometimes he had his son at the house with him. Ted had had a really tough time since his divorce. He also had some family problems that were going on with his sister."

I nodded, trying to look as if I didn't already know that information from Burton. Ted's sister had been blackmailed and then Hattie had, too. No wonder he'd been angry with Jonas.

"His sister was one of Jonas's victims. And then *I* was. So it seemed like Ted's life was really being totally hijacked by Jonas." Hattie shook her head. "I'll admit that I thought maybe Ted was the person behind Jonas's death. He was just so furious at him—animosity was practically seeping out through his pores when he talked about the guy. Then, suddenly, Jonas was dead. I couldn't help but think Ted might have been involved."

"And now you're thinking that he couldn't have been," I said.

"Exactly. Because if Ted killed Jonas, who killed Ted?"

I said, "Do you know how Jonas found out about your affair?"

Hattie made a face. "He seemed to have his fingers on the pulse of the town. He wasn't even living here for very long, so I'm not sure how he managed to know every bit of gossip in Whitby. But he told me he'd been driving by Ted's house and saw me slipping out. We tried to be careful, of course, but Jonas put it all together."

That was definitely unfortunate timing. I said, "Was it long before Jonas approached you?"

Hattie shook her head. "No. He showed up at the school to talk to me. I had no idea who he was and let him into my office, thinking he was a parent of one of the students. Then he started outlining what he'd seen and exactly what he wanted me to pay."

"I'm sure that was terrifying," I said.

"Awful. I was in such a panic that I could barely focus on what he was saying. I'm in the wrong industry to pay blackmailers. Being principal of the high school is a great job, but it doesn't pay enough for me for a lot of extras. And he was asking for a lot. I didn't want my husband to know about it so it was money I would need to come up with on my own." She paused, face reddening as she remembered. "He was so smug and self-satisfied. So slimy. I thought for a moment that I might strike him. Of course I didn't, though. I'm always so self-contained. And now things have gotten even worse and I'm a suspect in his murder."

Hattie's face was pale and her eyes looked tired. I asked, "Do you have an alibi? That would probably keep the police from seriously considering you as a suspect."

Hattie gave a short laugh. "I do, but I doubt it will be taken as a very good alibi. I was at home with my husband. The only problem is that I was so worried about Jonas blackmailing me that I couldn't sleep. I got up and went downstairs to do some work and try to wind down a little. So my husband can't exactly state he knows I was there the whole time. But of course I didn't kill anyone, not that I didn't want to. He brought a good deal of misery to me and, from what you said, to other people, too."

"Do you have any ideas about who might have wanted to harm Jonas?" I asked.

Hattie gave that short laugh again. "Everyone? Blackmailing is a dangerous business. If he'd set up shop extorting people, there must have been quite a few folks who wanted to get rid of him. And I totally get where they're coming from. My job would be in danger if I was found to have had an affair with the parent of a student—it simply would have served as a distraction. There's a very ambitious vice-principal who would love to have the school board promote her into my position."

"You mentioned the blackmailing to Ted, though?"

"Right. I had to tell somebody or I thought I was going to explode. Sort of like I'm telling you now. Although I have the feeling that the police aren't as interested in keeping my secret for me. Everyone is likely going to find out."

I said, "No wonder Ted was so angry at Jonas."

"That's right. Not only was his sister a victim of Jonas's, but I was, too. After I found out about Jonas's death, I was so worried that he was involved. I wanted to ask him right away but I couldn't find a moment away from my husband. Then Ted called me, which was *not* the way we usually communicated with each other. Ordinarily, we set up times to get in touch so that I would be alone. I had to step outside in the yard for a moment and tell my husband that a parent had called." She gave a short laugh. "Which happened to be the truth, now that I think of it."

"What did Ted say?"

Hattie said, "He told me that he had nothing to do with Jonas's death but he applauded whoever had. I admit that I didn't completely believe him—and I feel awful about that now. I'm wondering if maybe Ted had some inklings about who was responsible for murdering Jonas. Maybe he knew something."

"Did he seem to be a little secretive? Like he might be holding back on information?" I asked. I had thought the same thing when I'd had that conversation with Ted at the garage, but I didn't know him as well as Hattie did.

"I'm not really sure." She paused. "He started to tell me something on the phone, but stopped himself. Maybe he didn't want me to be in any danger by knowing who he suspected. I'd definitely gotten the impression something wasn't quite right. But I was so panicked about the possibility that our affair was going to become public knowledge that I didn't push him on it. The sad thing is that he and I both laid low after Jonas died. We didn't make contact with each other because we were worried our relationship was going to come to light. Now I really regret the distance between us. I still had feelings for Ted, even though I was trying to improve my marriage and be a more devoted partner."

A student was heading my way and I said quickly, "Sorry, it looks like there's a patron that might need my help."

Hattie immediately nodded and said, "Thanks, Ann. You've been a good listener." She headed back to the quiet study section.

Chapter Nine

I helped the student get connected to a research website on one of the library computers and to print out some materials she needed for a paper she was writing. When she seemed like she could pick it up from there, I headed back to the desk.

I looked up as the library doors opened. I smiled at the harried-looking middle-aged woman who came in with her cheerful mother and a slouching teen. "Hi, Ramona."

Ramona came in a couple of times a week to take her daughter to tutoring and her mother, Denise, to find a book. She prompted her daughter to head over to where the tutor sat waiting and then came over to chat. "Hi there, Ann."

"How are things going?" I asked.

It was a loaded question. Ramona rolled her eyes and said, "Well, I'm hanging in there. It's been quite a week over at my place."

"I know you stay busy over there."

Ramona said, "Oh yeah. There's the usual carpooling and driving around to activities and doctor appointments. But there's been extra added excitement recently. We live on the same street as the fella who was murdered."

"Jonas Merchant? That must really have made things a little crazier than usual," I said.

"Believe me, it has. Don't get me wrong; I love watching cop dramas on TV."

Ramona's mother chimed in, "Boy, does she. Every time I talk with her, she's watching something. British, American, Swedish. Anything she can find."

Ramona said, "But it's very different when the police are talking with *you*."

"I guess they were trying to find out if you'd seen or heard anything?" I asked.

Ramona nodded and looked wistful. "And I didn't see or hear a thing that really stood out. It made me so sad because I'd love to be one of those amazing witnesses who goes to the courtroom and really makes an impact. Somebody with total recall, you know? Instead, the whole morning and the night before was just a blur."

Denise said, "I helped you piece it together, though. You took Madison to volleyball practice the night before. And that next morning, you drove carpool. And you had to return to the school because Madison had forgotten to bring her homework with her."

Judging how unhappy Madison always looked when she was meeting her tutor, I had the feeling she wasn't a very enthusiastic student.

Ramona said, "Right, Mom. Unfortunately, it didn't really help me out when it came to reconstructing what might have happened at Jonas's house." She leaned toward me and said in a confidential tone, "Frankly, everybody on the street was glad to be done with him. He was pretty miserable as a neighbor."

"Really?" I asked, hoping she might fill in a little more information.

Denise said with a sniff, "Very disrespectful of older people."

"He yelled at my mom for not driving fast enough," said Ramona, sounding huffy.

"The speed limit is thirty-five," said Denise. "That means the *limit* is thirty-five miles per hour. Jonas used to fly through the neighborhood at complete disregard for any people walking or dogs or small children. It was completely disgraceful."

"As you can see, Mom was not a fan of his," said Ramona dryly. "There were plenty of other reasons, too. He never kept his yard up, for one. I can't tell you how excited the whole neighborhood is that *Flora*, of all people, is going to take on that property. Talk about a 180-degree difference! We go from somebody who didn't even mow his grass to a master gardener. So exciting. She was outside today planting flowers around the mailbox. Just a *beautiful* display of color. I tell you, that yard is going to look like the difference between night and day in just a few days. Sort of like one of those makeover shows on TV." She gave us a confiding look. "I think my neighbor, Reggie, is very interested in Flora. Won't they make a cute couple? He's so intellectual and she's so outdoorsy. I think they'd be a perfect match."

Ramona's mom crinkled her brow. "Reggie? Next door to Jonas's house?"

"The very one," said Ramona.

"I thought he played a different game," she said slowly.

"Played a different game? What do you mean, Mom?"

"Oh, what's the term? I thought he wouldn't be interested in Flora."

I asked, "You thought he 'played for the other team'?"

She beamed at me. "Exactly!"

Ramona was shaking her head. "I don't think so, Mom. He's definitely being flirty with Flora."

Denise's brow crinkled. "But I keep seeing that young man over there at his house."

"What young man?"

"Oh, I can't come up with his first name. He's a student at the college. He's Brenda Richards' son."

Ramona said, "Steven?"

"That's right. Steven. He pops by there all the time."

"Well, he must be over there to get some tutoring or something. For one thing, I can promise you he's interested in Flora. For another, he wouldn't be pursuing a relationship with a student of his." She turned back to me again. "Speaking of Reggie, he did have a terrible time with Jonas. Like I said, we were all going crazy over the state Jonas's yard was in. Reggie, being next door to him, got it the worst, really. He was brave and actually brought it up with Jonas. The rest of us just talked about Jonas's yard behind his back."

I said, "Jonas was hard to deal with, face-to-face?"

"Awful," said Ramona promptly. "I went over to give him a piece of my mind for speaking to my mom that way. He snarled at me and slammed the door in my face." She looked indignant at the memory.

Denise said, "And Jonas wasn't nice to that girl he was dating, either. What was her name? Octavia?"

"Augusta," said Ramona, nodding. "And you're right. I just about called Burton a couple of times, what with the yelling I heard going on inside that house."

I blinked. "You could hear them from your house?"

"Well, not from *inside* my house. But since I *do* take care of my yard, I'd be out there pulling weeds or planting and I could hear the ruckus from Jonas's house. He wasn't too particular about closing his windows, even when he was having an argument. Those two fought about everything; I can't imagine how they ended up being a couple."

Ramona's mom said crisply, "That other woman was over there, too. That set me to wondering if Jonas and Augusta were arguing because of that woman being over there."

"Hattie? From the high school?" asked Ramona. "You were telling me about that, Mom. But I don't think she was there as Jonas's romantic interest. She's married, for one thing. Plus, she was really angry." She looked at me. "His windows were open again and Hattie's voice carries."

"In education, you need a voice that carries," said Denise, bobbing her head, approvingly. "What was she mad about? Jonas's yard, like everyone else?"

Ramona shook her head. "No. Something to do with him spying on her. That sounds sort of crazy, doesn't it?"

"Not really," said Ramona's mom with a sniff. "After all, he was paying a lot of attention to my driving. Which is *excellent*, by the way."

Ramona gave me an eye-roll. "Right. Okay, well, we'd better find us some books, Mom. Ann, we'll see you in a little while."

The rest of the day went by rather quietly. In between helping patrons, I was able to get some work done and Fitz was able to get some napping done—some of it in my lap at the reference desk while I rubbed him from time to time.

The next morning, I slept in a little bit since I wasn't scheduled to work. It was always so nice to wake up on my own and without having the alarm blaring at me. Although I hadn't woken up *entirely* on my own. I'd had a little furry creature purr in my ear as if to remind me that his tummy rumbles informed him it was time to wake up.

I got out of bed, did some stretching, and fed Fitz first. Then I decided to go ahead and put on my athletic clothes so I could get some exercise in before I took my shower. It was always my goal to try to do a little exercising every day because my job was often on the sedentary side of things. But sometimes things didn't quite work out that way. On the days I opened the library, I found it hard to get up early enough to exercise first—and then, after work, I was sometimes too tired mentally to do it.

I was stepping out my front door when I saw Grayson there, his hand raised to knock. He gave me a rueful look. "Oops. Have I missed you again?"

"Not a bit. I was just going to take a walk around the neighborhood—want to join me?"

Grayson was already ready for a day at the newspaper office, wearing khaki pants and a button-down shirt. He grimaced. "I have a staff meeting first thing. Can I just walk with you for a couple of minutes and then head back?"

"Sure. We'll make sure we're not going fast enough for you to work up a sweat."

I felt glad that he hadn't come by a few minutes later or he'd have missed me completely. I was going to start seeming very elusive. We set out down the street.

"You must have the day off today," said Grayson with a smile.

I grinned at him. "Because I'm not in a mad scramble to get to the library? Correct. Considering I was there late last night, it's good to have a quiet morning. How did everything go with the dinner at your friend's house last night?"

"It was good," said Grayson. "I missed you, though. We'll have to do it another time."

One of his friends had apparently been playing his playlist for everyone and he had discovered some new music. Grayson pulled it up on his phone and we listened as we walked. Then he said, "I'm sure you heard about Ted."

I nodded. "Burton came by the library to let me know and to get filled in on anything I'd heard."

Grayson shook his head. "Such a tragedy. He was a great guy. He seemed really close to his son, too. I feel for him—that's a tough age to lose a father, when you're trying to make sense of your teen years."

"I know. It was a real shock." I paused. "I was thinking back to our conversation with Ted when we were at the garage. I felt at the time that Ted might be holding back some information. Did you get the same impression?"

Grayson thought it over and then slowly shook his head again. "I don't think I did, no. I mean, *now* I think he must have known something and that's why he was murdered. But at the time, I don't think I picked up on that fact."

We came up on Jonas's old house and saw Flora out in the yard. There were a couple of piles of garbage bags stacked up near the front door. She spotted us and gave us a wave as we walked over.

"Hi Flora," I said. "Looks like you're doing a lot of work this morning. Do you know my friend, Grayson Phillips?"

They shook hands and Grayson's eyes crinkled at her. "Good to meet you."

"Likewise," said Flora with a smile. She turned to me and said, "Unfortunately, the state of Jonas's house and yard were calling out to me. I decided I should get an early start before it got hot outside. I know nothing has gone through probate yet, but I thought the neighbors might appreciate the effort, especially with the yard. It seemed like a good use of my day off today."

Grayson looked at his watch and said ruefully, "Sorry, but I've got to head back now for that meeting. Flora, it was good to meet you. See you later, Ann."

"Nice meeting you," said Flora.

I saw she'd already done some weeding, picked up sticks and other yard debris, and had raked out a couple of beds. "I'm sure the neighbors do appreciate it, Flora. You've already accomplished a ton."

"Well, not as much as I'd like to. Sometimes when you're clearing something out, it makes you want to do *more*. It's like you realize how much farther you have to go. Plus, I'm working on clearing out the inside of the house, too."

I nodded at the bags. "Looks like you're making some headway."

Flora sighed. "There's still a ton more work to do. Jonas hadn't cleared out anything from when our dad died. Dad was something of a packrat, so there are old catalogs, old mail, newspapers, coupons he didn't use, and tons of old clothes. Instead of getting rid of stuff, Jonas just added a bunch more stuff. Plus, I don't think he weeded through his own things before he moved in because there's a lot of junk that I know was Jonas's. It's just a real mess."

I said, "Just remember that there's no deadline for knocking this out. Take your time and pace yourself. I remember when I was clearing out my great aunt's cottage before I moved in. It was hard for a lot of different reasons."

A face appeared in the window at the front of the house and I could see an engagingly ugly mutt grinning at us.

"Looks like somebody is doing pretty well," I said lightly.

Flora turned around to follow my gaze and chuckled. "Hi there, Bandit. Is it okay if I bring him out for a minute to say hello? I'm working on getting him better socialized. Jonas didn't do a great job with that." Her tone indicated that she thought Jonas hadn't done a good job with much.

I nodded and Flora brought Bandit out on a leash. He immediately threw himself on his back for a tummy rub and I was happy to oblige.

"Good boy," I murmured to him and his tongue lolled out the side of his mouth happily as his eyes closed halfway.

Flora smiled down at us. "He looks good, doesn't he? He's really a very bright boy and eager to please. Bandit is *so* relieved to be getting this much attention. I think he must have been attention-starved when he was with Jonas." Her face darkened at the thought.

"Well, I know he's delighted to be hanging out with you," I said.

"Yeah. We're buddies now, aren't we, Bandit? The nice thing about my work is they have no problem with me bringing a dog there. I brought him yesterday and he just trotted around behind me the whole way, saying hi to customers and helping me set out the new plants we'd gotten in."

"That sounds like the perfect arrangement," I said.

"Definitely. I was so relieved that Bandit was so good because I was going to feel awful about leaving him at my apartment all day while I worked. But it seems like he's really adjusted to life with me. I'm working on getting him better with the leash, though. Jonas apparently never took him on walks so Bandit doesn't really understand the concept. It's going to take some practice. Plus lots of treats."

I grinned at her. "I have the feeling you're not going to have any problem training him if you're using treats."

"So far, so good! At least he's happy with me holding onto the leash now, although we're not walking. That wasn't the case when I first tried it on him." She paused and then said, "I could use a little more coffee. Would you like to come in and see the progress I've made with the house?"

I asked, "I won't be in the way?"

"Oh, no. Actually, it might help to keep me motivated to show you what I've done. Like I said, all I can think about is how much farther I have to go."

So I followed Flora and Bandit inside. The house was a little bigger than my cottage, although not by much. I could see why Flora thought of it as a major project. The interior was dimly-lit and sort of gloomy and there were piles of catalogs and boxes against walls.

Flora followed my gaze and sighed. "Yes, the boxes. Those are all of Jonas's things. It makes it look like he'd just moved in, but he'd been here for over a year. He should have realized if he hadn't used the stuff in the boxes in a year that he didn't need it at all and just given it away."

I glanced around the living room. "I bet you've cleared out a lot, Flora. There aren't any boxes against these two walls and I have the feeling there were before you started clearing."

Flora brightened. "You're right. I figured I'd do the living room and the kitchen first and then move on to the other rooms."

She led us on a short tour of the house. "Excuse our progress," she said wryly. "Isn't that what stores that are under construction always put on signs?"

I could see why Flora felt overwhelmed. As we went toward the back of the house, there was even more stuff. There were piles of newspapers and catalogs and papers stacked against the walls in the back bedrooms. Flora said, "My dad never let me clean up while I was taking care of him. I was itching to go through those papers and toss them. But he wouldn't hear of it. I figured what I'd do is to sort things into trash and giveaway piles, so that's mostly what I've been doing. But being in this house can bring me down, so I've also been taking breaks to go outside and do yardwork. That's my happy place." Flora paused and then added, "Something else that's been bringing me down is that I heard there's been another death in town."

I nodded. "Ted Hill. Did you know him?"

"Not well. Only because he kept my beat-up car going and because he didn't live far from my place. I just can't believe there's been another murder." She looked grim. "My duplex apartment isn't far from Ted's house. My neighbor was saying the police took out a baseball bat as if it was evidence. That's really sad if it's the murder weapon because it's probably his son's bat. I'd see his son outfitted for baseball all the time when he was staying with his dad."

The baseball bat was new information. Of course, it was gossip, so it needed to be taken with a grain of sand.

We walked back to the kitchen. "I'm going to pour that coffee I was talking about. Would you like some?"

I nodded and soon we were sitting down at the kitchen table with two steaming mugs of coffee in front of us.

Flora was clearly still musing on the same line of thought. "And, even as early as it is, the police have already been by to speak with me. I guess they must think Ted's death is somehow related to Jonas's. Obviously, they think I'm a suspect in my brother's death, so I guess it follows that I'm one in Ted's."

I said, "I'm sure it's just standard procedure. I wouldn't read too much into it, Flora. I'm guessing they have to follow-up on the original interviews they conducted."

Flora said wryly, "I'd like to believe you. But it seems to me like the police believe I wanted to get rid of Jonas in order to get this house." She looked around her. "In its current condition, it's hard to believe they'd consider that a motive." She rubbed her eyes, looking exhausted. "I'm going to tell you something, Ann, but maybe you could keep it under your hat."

"Of course I will."

"When the police were searching the house, they found evidence that Jonas was blackmailing people." Flora made an expression of distaste. "I don't know if I'll ever be able to look those folks in the eyes again."

"I'm so sorry, Flora. That must have been a real shock. But his victims know you weren't involved in it. You shouldn't feel uncomfortable around them."

Flora sighed. "I hope you're right. I just feel like my brother has created this enormous problem for everybody. First off, Jonas embarrassed them by bringing their secrets to light. Then he blackmailed them. Then he died and they're being treated like suspects who might be carted off to jail at any point."

"How do you think Jonas got the information that he was blackmailing people with?"

Flora said, "I'm afraid I know exactly how he did. My dad. My father, bless his soul, was a gossipy old guy. He loved just sitting outside at the coffee shop and listening to the conversations of others. No one ever looked at him as any sort of threat because he seemed completely harmless. But he knew *everything* about everybody. He'd listen to people gossiping about other people. He'd eavesdrop on people talking about their own lives and issues."

"And then he'd pass that information along to your brother?"

"Exactly. Oh, it wasn't a malicious thing. Dad had no idea what Jonas was planning on doing with the information. He was simply pleased that Jonas was interested in hearing what he had to say—he didn't think there was any sort of motive behind it. Dad was very naïve about Jonas. He wasn't the son he thought he was, nor the man—here we are with Jonas dead because he was blackmailing people and Dad's own daughter is a suspect."

I said, "As you mentioned, the blackmail victims do have a pretty strong motive."

Flora shrugged. "But some people will still think I killed Jonas for this house. Sadly, Jonas wasn't worth going to jail over, house or no house. Although he really did aggravate me by his behavior." She shook her head. "Anyway, enough of all that. Let's talk about something different. You and Grayson, for instance. Are the two of you just friends?"

I could feel myself coloring a little. I shook my head. "We've been dating for a while now."

Flora gave me a smile. "I thought that might be the case. There was definitely a spark between the two of you. Congratulations to you for finding someone to date in Whitby. That's not the easiest thing in the world."

"Is there someone special for you?"

Flora shook her head. "Nope. It's fine—I've gotten used to being alone by now, and I kind of like it. I'm really routine-driven and set in my ways, so it would probably be tough for me to adapt to being in a relationship. Anyway, I'm pretty much an introvert, I guess. I like hanging out with my plants. And with Bandit, too, now." She reached down to rub the dog, who grinned up at her, lovingly.

"I understand being an introvert," I said. "I like staying inside and quiet most of the time, too."

"But Grayson . . . I got the impression he might be more of an extrovert. Being a journalist, I suppose that goes with the territory, doesn't it? You have to be outgoing to be able to track down stories, make cold calls, and do interviews."

"True. And you don't necessarily have to be extroverted to work at a library," I said with a smile. "Although I have a coworker who's a major extrovert."

Flora looked thoughtful. "There is one guy who I'm not so sure about."

"About whether he's an introvert or extrovert?"

"Oh, I'm pretty sure he's an introvert. But I just can't figure out what his motives are," said Flora.

"His motives?" I raised my eyebrows.

"That's right. It's Reggie Bartlett, from next door. He's a professor over at the college. Do you know him?"

I nodded. "He comes by the library quite a bit."

"I'm sure he's probably just delighted that I'm over here working on the yard since it's been horrible for years. It's just that he's over here at the house quite a bit when I'm here. It could be a coincidence. He seems like a kind of quiet guy, but he keeps popping over which makes me wonder if maybe he's more extroverted than he seems. Reggie even gave me a cutting from one of the plants in his yard."

"It sounds to me like he's flirting with you," I said. I was positive of it, in fact, judging from what I'd seen when I was last over here. Reggie had only had eyes for Flora.

"Do you think so?" asked Flora, pursing her lips uncertainly.

"Positive."

Flora said slowly, "I'm just not sure. We're in totally different lines of work. Plus, I'm a lot older than he is."

"Yes, but Reggie has always seemed like an old soul to me. Besides, it looks like he's interested in gardening and the state of his yard, so he might have more in common with you than you think."

Right at that moment, there was a tap at the door and Bandit made a few excited barks. Flora frowned. "Who could that be?"

I raised my eyebrows again and smiled.

Chapter Ten

Sure enough, it was Reggie . . . I saw him through the window in the door. Flora turned and gave me a wink before she opened the door.

She said, "Hi, Reggie! Would you like to come in? I'm just visiting with my friend Ann for a few minutes. You know Ann, don't you?"

Reggie, looking a little flustered, said, "Oh, hi Ann. I hope I'm not disturbing anything."

"No," I said. "I was literally just walking by and Flora was kind enough to invite me in. Actually, I should probably be heading out on my walk now."

But the look Reggie shot me was full of panic as if he wanted me there to make it all easier. Flora looked a little unsure, too.

"But," I added, "I'd like to hear how things are going with you, too, Reggie. I'll stay for a few minutes before I continue on my walk."

"Would you like some coffee, Reggie?" asked Flora politely.

"Hmm? Oh, no thanks. I've already had my daily allowance for the day." He set down a tote bag he was carrying and sat at the table with us. Now it was his turn to look a bit unsure.

"Flora, I was in the store yesterday afternoon and saw this." He pulled out a welcome mat that stated *welcome* with an exclamation point after the word. "I thought it might be a nice housewarming gift for you."

I hid a smile. It looked like wishful thinking to me. Reggie wanted to be especially welcome at Flora's new place.

"That's so sweet of you! Jonas didn't have a mat at all outside so this will be perfect. I keep finding myself tracking in mud after I've been working in the yard."

This being said, neither of them looked very sure about what they should say next. They glanced my way and I quickly said, "Reggie, how have things been going at the university? What classes are you teaching now?"

Flora added, "Yes, I was wondering the same thing. I keep thinking that I wish I could be back in school again—I'd treat the whole experience so much differently."

Reggie smiled at her and asked, "What kinds of things would you change?"

Flora flushed a little and laughed. "Well, I'd probably spend more time studying and less time partying with friends, for one. But for another, I'd choose different classes. Heck, I'd choose a whole different major, as a matter of fact."

I asked, "Your major wasn't related to horticulture?"

Flora snorted. "You've seen the yard out there. It was almost that bad when Dad was still alive. He wasn't at all interested in plants and didn't think it was a real job. He wanted me to go into accounting. So I was taking business and accounting courses."

Reggie nodded thoughtfully. "I've seen the same thing happen a lot with my students. They'll want to have a history degree or an English degree and their parents want them to choose something practical. But I've always thought history and English degrees *were* practical because they taught you how to write well and writing well is important for a lot of different jobs."

Flora asked, "What happens to the kids whose parents wanted them to choose a different major?"

"I always feel bad for them. They really feel a pull to please their parents, who are often helping to pay for their education. But you can see they're really torn. Sometimes they meet with their advisor and make the change to the major *they* want. But sometimes they keep on with the engineering degree or the accounting degree or whatever it is that their parent wants. Sometimes it works out and sometimes it doesn't. How did your dad react when you decided to pursue horticulture?"

Flora gave him a rueful look. "Let's just say he wasn't exactly pleased. But to be honest, he wasn't really going to be pleased no matter what I did." She seemed to want to change the subject. "What classes are you teaching?"

Reggie smiled at her. "I'm teaching a variety of different classes right now, from the lower-level 101 and 102 history courses to global diplomacy in the modern world. There is an ancient civilization class, too."

"What's your favorite to teach?" I asked.

He considered this a moment. "It varies, depending on the day. But mostly I like the ancient civ class. That might be because the students in it are really engaged and interested in the material, which makes it a very lively class. Considering it takes place directly after lunch, that's surprising."

I laughed. "I remember trying to stay awake in most of my post-lunch classes. Depending on the class, it could be a challenge."

Reggie glanced around him and said, "Speaking of challenges, Flora, it looks like you've been working really hard here."

She smiled at him. "I was telling Ann that most of my work is evident in the kitchen and living room right now. The back of the house is still a major disaster area. Actually, most of the house is still a major disaster area, but I'm trying to see the positives. I'm taking it as it comes, but prioritize the living areas."

Reggie nodded. "That's what they say. The best way to eat an elephant is one bite at a time. I've noticed you've made a ton of progress with the yard."

Flora chuckled. "It's been a long time coming, hasn't it? Thanks—I'm trying. Right now, I'm in the stage where I'm just trying to clear out debris and remove some of the old beds. Then I'm going to do some major planting. Hopefully it's going to be a lot more presentable soon."

Reggie flushed a little. "I think it looks really presentable now. Honestly, just having it be neat and tidy was most of what it needed. I didn't mean that you should do a complete revamp. My own yard isn't all that great. I wish I had more time to work in it, but I have to prioritize."

I said, "Oh, Flora is a master gardener. She's probably been itching to get her hands on the property."

Flora nodded ruefully. "That's exactly right. Dad never wanted anything changed inside or outside the house and I was always dying to clean things up. Then Jonas moved in and the place really went to pot. I've always dreamed of how nice I could make the yard."

Reggie asked Flora about her work at the nursery, so they chatted about that for a few minutes with Reggie asking questions and Flora happily answering them. Once again, I felt like I should duck out but I had the feeling that it might make things awkward between them.

"Do you have any hobbies?" Flora asked Reggie politely.

"I do, not that I have a lot of time to spend on them. I'm afraid they're not so much centered around gardening, although I'd love to learn more about horticulture. I play chess online, for one and I also have a classic car my dad gave me that I'm trying to work on from time to time."

Then the conversation's direction took a sudden detour from hobbies when Reggie hesitantly said, "I was wondering, Flora, if you'd had a visit from the police?"

I hid a smile. Reggie seemed to have trouble with conversational transitions. I supposed a lot of his interactions with people revolved around the classroom and not regular social situations.

"About Ted Hill's death? Yes, I have. I think the police must be speaking with everyone they interviewed after Jonas died. Actually, Ann and I were just talking about it. Did you know him?"

Reggie nodded. "Actually, I knew him a little bit because his son was interested in getting a tour of the college. He's not at the point of applying yet, but he's in that stage where he's doing college visits and trying to figure out where he might *want* to apply.

Ted knew that I worked there and asked if I could give his son and him a tour of the campus."

I said, "That was nice of you. Usually the admissions office handles that, right?"

"Exactly. But I love Whitby College and figured I'd make a good ambassador for it, even though I only know it from the academic side." He sighed. "And then the police came by yesterday to find out what I was doing when Ted died. It makes me sad to think that I'm somehow a suspect. Plus, once again I don't have a ready-made alibi. It seems that I spend too much time at my house."

Flora smiled at him approvingly. She definitely fancied introverts.

Reggie gave Flora an apologetic look. "I wanted to make sure you knew, as well, that although I had my . . . differences . . . with Jonas, I would never harm him or *anyone* in any way. That's not a good way to resolve conflicts. I'm a man of words and I might have shared quite a few words of displeasure with Jonas, but that's as far as it went."

She smiled at him. "I never thought you could have been involved. And I'm just like you—my brother drove me absolutely insane, but I'd never do anything to hurt him. It's just not in my nature." She paused. "What do you think about Ted's death?"

Reggie shook his head. "It's baffling to me. I didn't know him, of course. I understand he was the guy who I saw at Jonas's house that day. All I keep thinking is that he must have known something about what happened to Jonas. Is that what you both think?"

I said, "I can't think of another reason why someone would want to harm Ted."

Flora added, "I figured he must have either seen or heard something. Or maybe he simply put the pieces together with information he already had."

I said to Reggie, "Have you thought any more about who might have killed Jonas? If we know that, it sounds like we might end up knowing who was responsible for Ted's death."

Reggie said, "Well, I've been thinking a little bit more about Jonas and Augusta's relationship. That was the woman he was seeing shortly before he died. Their relationship was pretty fiery. Sometimes I'd sit outside on my patio to grade papers and get a little Vitamin D and I could hear them arguing inside the house."

"Did it ever get violent?" I asked.

"Not as far as I could tell. I'd have intervened if I thought it was. I'd definitely have called the police. It seemed to me like a lot of bickering followed by yelling matches." He colored a little bit and said, "I hope you both don't think I was a nosy neighbor. It was genuinely hard not to overhear."

Flora said quickly, "I'm sure it was. Plus, it must have been very aggravating trying to work while people were arguing so loudly. Jonas sounds like he must have been the worst neighbor in history."

Reggie chuckled, "Well, it was a bit of a challenge sometimes, but not too bad. That's what I was telling the police. I knew both victims, of course, so they had lots of questions for me." He looked at Flora. "Did you think your brother's relationship with Augusta was rocky, too?"

"From the little I was able to gather? Yes. Unfortunately, I wasn't really welcome over at the house so it wasn't as if I could really observe the two of them together very often. I know that Jonas had ended that relationship and was dating someone else, though—my friends saw Jonas out with a different woman a couple of different times. Since Jonas and I weren't close, so I really didn't know much about Augusta." She sighed. "I wish things had been different. I always felt sort of alone in my family."

Reggie hesitated and then said, "Your mom has been gone for a while?"

"She died in a car accident when Jonas and I were both teenagers."

I said gently, "That must be a really hard time to lose your mom."

Flora nodded. "It was. She was great, too. Mom was the one who took us to school and listened to how our days had gone. She kept up with doctor and dentist appointments and set up carpools for our different after-school activities. Once she was gone, Dad just wasn't the right guy to be a solo parent. Jonas and I really had no emotional support from him. Worse, he acted as if nothing had happened . . . like we hadn't even lost Mom. He never spoke about her after she died. The only time he acknowledged things had changed was when he asked me to step in and take over the cooking and keeping up the house."

Reggie made a face. "He didn't ask your brother to chip in?"

"I'm afraid Dad was not exactly a forward thinker." She sighed. "I guess he tried his best. At any rate, I grew up unscathed, although I guess the same can't be said for Jonas. If

Mom had still been around, I don't think he'd have grown up as twisted as he did. He and Mom had been really close."

Suddenly tiring of the subject, Flora quickly said, "Let's talk about something a little more cheerful. Ann, why don't you tell us what's going on at the library? Reggie, I don't know if that's a place you often visit, but there are so many great programs over there."

Reggie brightened. "I'm over there all the time."

They smiled at each other, feeling that connection again.

After pitching some of the upcoming programs and continuing to visit for a few minutes, I decided to try to gratefully exit. Bandit whined as I stood up and Flora asked the dog, "Need to go potty?" Bandit dangled his tongue from his mouth and grinned at her.

Reggie quickly leaped into action. "I'll take him out real quick."

Flora's lips quirked into a smile. "Okay, thanks."

He attached a leash to Bandit's harness and followed me outside. "Hey Ann," he said quickly, "You know Flora pretty well, don't you?"

I shrugged. "Pretty well. We've been friends for a while—we get coffees together sometimes or grab lunch."

Reggie cast a quick look behind him to make sure Flora hadn't followed us out. "Do you have any tips at all? If I'd like to go out with Flora, I mean."

I hid a smile. Reggie, despite being quite the academic, was about as clueless as a teenager when it came to dating. I said slowly, "Tips? You mean, like the best place for you to go on a date? That kind of thing?"

He nodded, looking a little shy. "Exactly. Or do you know what Flora's type might be?"

I couldn't hold back the grin anymore. "The only tip I really have is to be yourself. And maybe make the first date something really casual, like a coffee or drinks or something. Just see how it goes."

Bandit started pulling toward the house and Reggie said, "Thanks, Ann. Maybe you could talk me up a little to her, too?"

"I'll see what I can do."

I hesitated and then said, "Hey, I'm going to have a get-together on Saturday afternoon. I'm planning on inviting Flora. Maybe you should come."

Reggie gave me a boyish smile. "Really? Sure, that might make things easier. Thanks!"

Reggie went back inside with Bandit, a bounce in his step, and I continued my walk around the neighborhood.

Chapter Eleven

As I strode around the neighborhood, I thought about Grayson and me. I remembered being just as awkward around him before we started dating—maybe even more so. My previous dating experiences had never gone very well and I'd been in a horrible cycle of ghastly blind dates before Grayson moved to the neighborhood. Even after he moved in, it took a long while for anything to really develop between us. Now, it was hard to imagine a day without Grayson in it.

I knew we were both very different from each other in a lot of ways. Opposites do tend to attract. In a lot of ways, it's probably good for me to push myself a little bit—to meet new people, do new things, and go to new places with Grayson. The only problem is trying to mesh our two different personalities into a relationship that works. I decided I'd give him a call later on and see if we could plan a time when I could properly meet his friends, since I'd bowed out from going with him to the dinner one of them was hosting. I'd briefly met one or two of them when Grayson was out, but it wasn't as if I'd really spent time talking to them. I figured it might be a little easier for me if meeting them was on my home turf and I was the one hosting.

Once I got back home, I decided to do a little yard work since I was sweaty from my walk anyway. Maybe Flora inspired me to tackle some of my front yard. Weeding wasn't my favorite thing in the world, but I realized if I did a little bit every week then it didn't get out of control. Jonas's yard was definitely a warning about what could happen when things got out of control. So I yanked the dandelions, clover, and chickweed up with impunity into a pile and then tossed them in my compost bin as Fitz watched me with interest from a sunny spot on the window sill.

Then I went inside, loved on the cat for a few minutes, and headed to the shower to get cleaned up. After that, it was my favorite time of day—curling up with my book on the sofa with Fitz and a cup of chai tea next to me. The little bit of exercise followed by the comfort of a good book and good company helped me completely relax.

I couldn't spend all day doing that, though, unfortunately, although I certainly gave it a go. After a couple of hours, I gingerly moved off the sofa as Fitz gave me a slightly indignant look. "Sorry, buddy," I said. "Laundry is calling."

Not just laundry, but plenty of other routine household tasks. Then I realized I had an errand to run if I wanted to make sure I had lunches to pack to take to work for the next few days. I carefully made a list before I went because I'd discovered how dangerous wandering aimlessly around a grocery store was for me. Dangerous for my wallet, that is.

I was in the produce aisle when my phone rang. I fumbled with my purse and nearly dropped the phone when I took it out. I glanced at it to see who was calling and grimaced. Zelda Smith.

It was never a good thing when Zelda was calling me. It meant that I'd unknowingly committed some homeowner association atrocity—maybe my grass was over regulation-height or there were some stray weeds poking up between the cracks in my driveway. I hesitated, wondering if I should just let the call go to voicemail and finish up my shopping. But the phone persistently kept ringing, sounding more and more aggravated.

Finally, I picked up. "Hello? Zelda?"

Zelda blew out a sigh of relief. "I was starting to think you weren't going to answer the phone." Her voice sounded accusatory.

"Sorry. I'm at the grocery store and it took me a while to get my phone out." Hopefully I wasn't going to be struck by lightning in the middle of the store for that lie.

Zelda made a harrumphing sound as if it was a poor excuse. "I need your help."

"What's happened?" Now I felt a bit guilty for avoiding Zelda. I shouldn't make assumptions about why people call me, even if they routinely phone to harangue me about something to do with my property.

"My car has broken down. It's extremely bad timing, of course. I heard about Ted Hill." Her voice made it seem as though Ted Hill had really inconvenienced her by dying the way he had.

"Where are you now? Did your car break down at home, or are you out on the road?"

"On the road," said Zelda impatiently, as if that must be self-evident. "I'm stuck here."

I glanced at my cart, which was full of refrigerated and frozen items and sighed. I wasn't done shopping yet so I didn't want to go ahead and check out or else I'd have to figure out a time to come back. "Okay. Where are you? I'm on my way."

Zelda was at a local department store not too far away. I left my cart with a store associate with a promise that I'd be back soon and headed out the door.

I drove slowly through the parking lot and pulled up next to a distinctive older-model car that was kept in pristine condition. Zelda was leaning up against the car with a dissatisfied look on her face.

"Hi there," I said lightly in what I hoped was a peppy voice. "Everything okay?"

Zelda shook her head sharply. "Everything is not okay. It's a very bad day."

Hearing my formerly-lovely day off pronounced a very bad day was decidedly sobering. "I'm sorry. Want to hop in my car? Should we call for your car to be towed?"

Zelda did no hopping, but she did take measured steps over to my vehicle and climbed in. She glared at her own car. "It won't start."

"I'm sorry," I said again. "I'd look under the hood, but I have absolutely no knowledge about cars whatsoever. Why don't we call the garage?"

Zelda's mouth twisted. "Who will answer? Ted Hill is dead now."

From Zelda's tone, it appeared that she found Ted's death very unacceptable and inconvenient.

"True," I agreed. "But he has a slew of mechanics and a tow driver working for him. He employed a lot of people. Surely the garage hasn't completely shut down—they were working on lots of customers' cars. Those people will need their cars back."

"I already called over there and nobody picked up." Zelda was looking petulant but I heard a hint of a tremor in her voice. Could it be that the unflappable Zelda might be about to break down?

I started up the car. "We can fix this. I'm sure it's pretty chaotic over at the garage with Ted gone—he was the one who handled the incoming phone calls. Let's just drive over there and see if we can speak to someone in person."

A look of relief passed over Zelda's features and I felt relieved, too. Relieved that I'd made some headway with her. I turned on the radio to the classical music station that the college ran so that we could have some background music as I headed to the garage. She did not seem to be in the mood for light chatting. Now that I thought of it, this must be a very difficult situation for Zelda to find herself in. She was used to being in charge and in control. It must be very tough for someone like her to feel vulnerable.

We got to the garage, parked, and went into the office. I could tell immediately that things had changed there since Ted's death. He kept the place neat and seemingly organized. Right now, however, the office exuded the kind of chaos that you might find after some sort of dystopian event. There were paper files everywhere, their insides spilling out onto the counter and the desk, the phone was ringing, and there was no one in the office.

Zelda grunted, her features settling into even more lines of malcontent. "Nobody to help."

"They're here, clearly," I said. "I'm going out into the service bay to find someone."

Zelda, ever the rule-follower, pointed at a large sign on the door leading out into the garage. "It says no one is allowed to go out there."

"Well, it wouldn't be necessary if someone was in the office. I'll be right back, Zelda."

There were dire mutterings going on behind me as I opened the door and stepped into the garage. I saw at once that there seemed to be chaos going on out there, too—the mechanics were snapping at each other, there were lots of cars lined up for service, and the cheerful music that I could usually hear emanating from the service bays was nowhere in evidence.

The sound of the various tools they were using was loud, so I raised my voice to be heard above it. "Hello? Can I get some help in the office?"

There was no response so I cleared my throat and spoke even louder, raising my tone to what sounded like a roar to my ears. "Can I get some help, please?"

Now the tools all stopped and the mechanics looked at me and then at each other. "I went last time," said one of them in a grumbling voice.

Another man gave a long-suffering sigh and hauled himself out from under a car. He didn't look happy at the prospect of transitioning from mechanic to customer service representative. "In the office," he muttered.

Zelda had her face pressed against the glass, watching the proceedings. She drew back as she saw us coming.

The man stepped behind the desk and looked at us with a tired expression on his grease-stained face. "What type of vehicle is it?"

Zelda snapped, "It's not even here. It broke down in front of the department store. Wouldn't start up."

The man sighed and rubbed a grease-stained hand against the side of his face. "Look, I've got to level with you. We're totally backed up here. The owner died and he handled all of the office-related stuff. We don't even have his login for the computer so we've had to dig out paper files. The whole thing is just a disaster."

I said, "Do you have a tow truck driver? The car needs to be moved from the parking lot, at least. We can worry about scheduling the repair to the vehicle later."

"Yeah, but the tow driver is like the rest of us—he's having to jump in to make repairs and then take a turn helping out in the office, too. It's a real mess because people are calling us up to check on their cars and we can't even grab the phone because we're trying to get through the backlog."

Zelda's mouth twisted as she thought something through. Then she said, "I can pick up phones."

The mechanic just looked at her, not knowing what to say. Admittedly, Zelda didn't look like anybody's idea of a very professional receptionist. Her voice was grating and it was clear that she would be needing a smoke break at some point in the near future.

The man said hesitantly, "To be honest, I don't even know who's going to pay you . . . or us. Ted was the one in charge of payroll. We're just working and assuming a lawyer or accountant or somebody is going to write us a check at some point."

Zelda said curtly, "It's important to have someone in the office picking up the phone. This is just chaos." Her gaze flickered over the folders and papers spread over the front counter and her lip curled.

The phone rang and Zelda reached over to pick up the receiver. "Ted Hill's garage," she said smoothly. Then she shoved folders and papers aside until she found a legal pad and a pen and she started taking notes.

"Currently, the garage is extremely backed up. Could you come in for an oil change next week, instead?" She shoved a few more papers around until a desk calendar appeared. She made a careful notation on a day the following week before ending the call with the customer.

Zelda raised her eyebrows at the mechanic.

A car horn blared from the garage and the mechanic turned around. One of the other guys motioned him impatiently to return to the repairs. He said hastily, "Okay, you've got the job. What's your name?"

"Zelda Smith." She regarded the mechanic coolly.

"Okay. I'm Zack. Good luck in here. Maybe the guys can actually focus on getting these cars taken care of now."

He started to walk back to the garage. I quickly said, "This is great, but Zelda's car is still stuck out at the department store." And it was starting to look as if I was going to be on the hook for giving her rides for the near future.

The mechanic shook his head. "Can't do a thing about it today, but the tow driver can get on it tomorrow. Maybe you can call the department store and explain the situation so they won't tow. Tell them we'll get it first thing tomorrow."

Zelda looked at me. "Can you pick me up later?" She asked the mechanic, "What time does the garage close?"

"The office closes at five."

"Can you pick me up then?" she asked me.

"Yes," I said. "But tomorrow might be a little more problematic with the hours I'm working."

A shrewd look came into Zelda's eyes. She said to the mechanic, "Look, it will benefit both of us if my car gets fixed quickly. If you send someone out to tow it and then fix it early tomorrow, I can promise you things will be a lot less chaotic over here." She cast her eyes over the cluttered counter with a look of horror.

"Welllll," said the mechanic in a doubtful tone, "I just don't know about that, ma'am. The problem is that we'd be putting your car ahead of other people."

Zelda raised her etched-on eyebrows. "Who's to know? I won't tell if you won't."

He nodded his head slowly. "Okay. It's a deal."

I left, hurrying back to the grocery store. I hoped the staff hadn't given up on me and restocked the stuff in my abandoned cart. Luckily, when I got there, I saw it waiting for me near the registers. I grabbed it and hurried through the rest of my shopping trip.

Fifteen minutes later, I was putting the groceries away at home as Fitz watched me with sleepy-eyed interest. I swore the cat smiled when I pulled out the cat food from a bag.

"You know I wouldn't forget you," I said to him with a smile. He reached out and lovingly rubbed his head against my arm.

My phone rang right after I finished putting everything away. I picked it up as I settled myself down on my sofa. "Grayson?" I asked.

"Hey there," he said. "I was just thinking about you and thought I'd give you a call while I was taking a break. Am I interrupting any errands or anything?"

I chuckled. "No, although I did finish them kind of late. My day was briefly hijacked by Zelda."

"Uh-oh. Did you have some kind of homeowner association violation? I know she was coming after me a couple of weeks ago because my mailbox was rusty."

I said, "Not this time, although she's certainly pointed out plenty of violations in the past to me. She actually had car trouble and was stranded over at the department store."

Grayson said, "She must have been relieved to have gotten you on the phone. It would have taken her forever to walk back to her house from there. And I have the feeling she's not the type to try to find a ride-share service."

"I think she *was* relieved, actually. Mostly because she couldn't get anyone over at the garage to give her a hand. She'd tried calling over there and no one had answered."

"Ooohhh. I didn't even think about that. I bet the garage wasn't running the way it normally does with Ted gone," said Grayson slowly.

"Exactly. She'd tried to get the front desk to send out a tow truck and nobody picked up. So I drove her over there and the next thing I know, she has a receptionist job at Ted's garage."

Grayson burst out laughing. "Really? Now, that's the way to take charge. It sounds like the kind of story I need to write up for the newspaper."

"Well, when you write a story about Zelda, I have the feeling it needs to be clear that she's the heroine. Anyway, now I'm on the hook for picking her up from the garage at five. The good news is that she ended up being able to pressure the mechanics to prioritize her car since she's going to be helping them out over there."

"Maybe having a job means she won't have enough time to harass us anymore over homeowner violations," said Grayson with a chuckle.

"True. The only downside is that she might not be quite as available to volunteer at the library. I have to admit she's something of a Super Volunteer, even if she scares the patrons a little bit. But when she's there, she's like a shelving machine. I have to wonder what she did for a living before she retired."

Grayson asked, "What do you think she might have done?"

"Switchboard operator? The receptionist job seemed to come easily to her."

Grayson said, "They haven't had switchboards for a while, have they? But I can see what you're saying. We'll have to ask her."

"Speaking of asking about things, I wanted to see if you think it would be a good idea for your friends to come to a cookout at my house." I said this a little more awkwardly than I had in my mind. I was obviously not used to hosting anything more than a person or two at my house. Throwing a party was completely outside of my wheelhouse.

Grayson sounded a little surprised, too. "You're thinking about hosting a cookout?"

"Sure. A little backyard barbeque. Nothing really fancy—we can sit around outside since I don't have a lot of room in the house. Maybe it can even be before the football game on Saturday?"

I was proud of myself for that one. Although I definitely didn't have a big enough house to host a football watching party, I could probably handle the pre-game.

Grayson paused. Then he said warmly, "Ann, that's awesome. But are you sure you want to do something on your weekend? I know it's pretty rare that you even get the weekend off."

Although part of me was definitely wanting to spend the weekend with Grayson, Fitz, and a book, I knew this was important to Grayson. Relationships were about giving and taking, after all. "Of course I want to. And frankly, I think it will probably make me feel a lot more comfortable doing this on my home turf."

"That makes sense. And it sounds great! I'll let the guys know. So . . . something like 12:30? It's a 2:00 game, I think. I'll make sure everybody brings stuff, too. They might eat more than you'd think and you shouldn't have to foot the bill for this all by yourself."

"Sure thing. And I'll supply the hamburgers and hot dogs." I was sounding a lot more confident than I actually felt. The last time I'd fired up the grill, I was grilling vegetables. And I seemed to remember they'd ended up fairly charred. Cooking inside was one thing; cooking outside was something very different. "You'll be there to help me out with the grill, right?"

"Absolutely. I'm not the *best* grill master, but I should be able to keep stuff from falling down around the coals, anyway. And thanks for this, Ann. I'm really looking forward to it."

When I hung up the phone, I had a warm feeling. I could hear Grayson's smile through the phone. I settled back into my book and, snuggling with Fitz, feeling content.

Chapter Twelve

Later, I set back out to pick up Zelda from her new job. I parked the car outside and waited for a moment, but she didn't come immediately out so I walked inside. I blinked at the difference in the office from this morning. Instead of a blizzard of paperwork and folders on the counter, everything was very neatly organized. Zelda was on the phone and held up her skinny index finger to me, which I took to mean that she was wrapping up the call soon.

She said crisply to the person on the other end, "Because of the owner's death, things are running slightly behind here at the garage. You *do* understand." There was no question in that statement nor any room for the person on the other end of the line to argue. "Then you'll need to either wait to bring in your car for two days or drop it off, understanding we're not going to be able to get to it until then." She made a note on the desk calendar and then, after another moment, she hung up.

"Zelda," I said, "you've given this place quite a transformation."

She lifted up her head and looked proud. "It's much better, although there are still a few things I'd like to change. Maybe tomorrow. There is also a pile of notes in Ted's tiny back office that need to be worked through." She picked up her purse and we walked out.

"How are things going with your car?" I asked.

Zelda sniffed. "Well, it was towed in and the men have taken a preliminary look at it. There's something to do with a starter and maybe some other odds and ends. At any rate, they have the parts and it will be taken care of tomorrow morning. Are you available to drive me to the garage tomorrow? I won't need a ride home."

I nodded. "I don't open up the library tomorrow because I'm scheduled to close up. What time do you need to be here?"

Zelda considered this, her henna-red head tilted to one side. "They open at 7:30, but I might want to be there a few minutes early. The office and waiting area are in dire need of some improvements. I'm going to bring in an extra coffee pot I have. And although Ted was organized, he had his own method of doing things. I'm going to bring in some of my own office supplies that I have for doing homeowner association business and change it."

"Well, I know they're very grateful at the garage. It was total chaos when we were there this morning and you obviously have the place totally under control now."

Zelda looked pleased by this. "Yes. Yes, I do." She was quiet for a minute and then she said, "I better pack myself some lunch for tomorrow. It's going to be a long day. I'm planning on volunteering at the library after I get off at 5:00."

"Without eating anything for supper first?" I had the instinctive feeling this would end up being a bad idea. A hungry

Zelda who was tired out from a long day of working might make for a grouchy Zelda. She was already grumpy enough without making things worse. "Are you sure that's what you want to do? You could always come volunteer another time."

Zelda looked at me through narrowed eyes. "I'm positive. When I say I'm going to do something, I do it. Besides, it won't take me long to get the shelving done. I'll be in and out of there in no time."

"You are very quick," I admitted. "Okay, if you're sure. We'd love to have you there. You do a fantastic job."

Zelda preened and I wondered how many people really complimented her on the various things she did. She had such a brusque and overbearing manner and tough exterior that it almost seemed like she was above needing praise when she clearly wasn't. I might not really appreciate all the work she did for the homeowner association because the way she went about it could be annoying—but the fact of the matter was that she did an excellent and necessary job for the neighborhood. She made sure our home values were in good shape by getting everyone to take care of their house and property.

As I drove Zelda back home, she gruffly regaled me with stories from her day. Good customers, bad customers, and the piles of paperwork. She seemed to take a lot of grim satisfaction from what she'd accomplished.

I dropped her off at home and then went back to my house for another quiet evening. I realized that, although I'd gone to the store, I hadn't really planned what I was going to eat. What was more, I didn't really seem to have the motivation to plan a meal from all the disparate parts of the foods I'd purchased, nor to cook it.

Which was why I was absolutely delighted when Grayson tapped on the door holding a bag of takeout and smiling at me.

I opened the door wide. "Oh my gosh. How did you know?"

He grinned modestly and said, "Newspaper editors have excellent intuition."

I decided that we'd pretend it was a real dinner that one of us had cooked. I threw a tablecloth over my small, round kitchen table, lit a candle, and we served ourselves Chinese takeaway on real plates. Grayson turned on some jazz music for the background and we were set.

"Long day?" Grayson asked me.

"You know, it was a *good* day, really. I got my errands done. I was able to relax for a while. I got to pat myself on the back for helping Zelda out and doing my good deed for the day."

Grayson chuckled. "It sounded like you did your good deed *twice*."

"True. There was the dropping-off of Zelda and then the picking-up of Zelda. My good deed tomorrow will be knocked out early because I'm taking her to the garage before I head to the library."

Grayson gave me a sympathetic look.

I swallowed down a big bite of my sesame chicken. "You'll be shocked to hear that it wasn't so bad."

"Are you just being generous?" He quirked an eyebrow at me.

"Not a bit. Well, I'm not going to say that Zelda didn't grate on my nerves this morning when I had to abandon my grocery cart and run over to help her out. But this afternoon, it was cool to see how much she'd managed to accomplish in a day. And she looked so proud of herself when she talked about everything she'd done."

Grayson nodded. "I think she's one of those people who's really driven by personal achievement."

"I mistakenly thought she was driven by how much trouble she could cause," I said wryly. "Anyway, she did really knock out a lot today. I was shocked at how quickly Ted's neat and tidy office descended into pandemonium."

Grayson passed me one of the eggrolls. "When you first mentioned that to me, I was surprised, too. But I have the feeling that Ted really separated out the business side from the garage. He didn't have an assistant manager there. He was the only person who was in charge of scheduling and bookkeeping."

I nodded. "One of the mechanics said they didn't even know the password for the computer."

"Zelda was able to crack it?"

"Apparently so. She seemed to be typing on it when I picked her up this afternoon." I shrugged. "At this point, I don't think I should underestimate her. But that's enough about me and my day. How did things go for you? Are you working on another article about Jonas and Ted?"

Grayson said, "I'm trying to. I did ask Flora if she wanted to give me a quote for the paper. I wasn't sure if she was going to do it or not, but she immediately told me she wanted to. She pretty much repeated what she'd said at Jonas's funeral service—that they'd been close as children and she appreciated the support she'd received from friends. She added that she hoped the police would find the perpetrator and bring some resolution about before there were any additional deaths."

I nodded. "It sounds like a great statement. I'm not too surprised she made it because she'd mentioned it worried her that people might think she'd killed her brother in order to get the house. It's smart of her to get ahead of that and address it."

We chatted a little about other stories Grayson was working on at the paper and I updated him on the library-related article I wrote for him as a recurring piece. Then I said, "You know, going back to the party I'm hosting."

Grayson raised his eyebrows. "It's a party now? I thought it was just going to be a get-together."

"Right. Except now that I think about it, it makes sense for me to expand my guest list."

"Does it?" Grayson asked doubtfully. "It sounds like that might make things even more stressful."

"That's what I thought, at first. But now I'm thinking that maybe it would be good for me to have some friends of mine there, too. It might help make me a little more relaxed."

Grayson frowned. "I don't want this to be something you have to worry over."

"Oh, it's not. Well, it probably is a *little*, but that's just because I don't ordinarily host people at all. Even though I'm hosting, I do think it'll be easier for me to be on home turf, like I was saying earlier. Anyway, having other folks there to talk with will probably make things easier. I'm not inviting a ton of people—but I'm thinking my coworkers, Flora, maybe a few neighbors. Besides, since I don't really do any hosting, I owe a lot of people a return invitation for all the times they've invited *me* to get-togethers and I haven't returned the favor."

"If you're sure about that," said Grayson, still sounding a little doubtful.

"If I'm going to do something, I might as well go all-out," I said, sounding to my ears a lot more confident than I actually felt.

After Grayson left later, my mind was whirling thinking about who to invite, when to invite them, the things I would need to buy, and how to keep it all in some sort of budget. I took out a notebook and jotted down ideas in order to get it all out of my head so that I could sleep that night. Fortunately, and surprisingly, I was able to sleep a lot harder than I thought I could.

The next morning, I got up early and immediately put my workout clothes on. I'd found I'd *definitely* exercise if I didn't have to change clothes to do it. Then I took Zelda to the garage and helped her carry in the different supplies and the coffeepot she'd brought with her. Having completed my duties, I headed off to the park to get a brisk walk in.

While I was stretching at a park bench, I heard someone softly call my name. I turned around and saw Linus there with his dog, Ivy. I grinned at my favorite patron and said, "Hi there, you two! How are you today?"

Ivy, a large dog of indeterminate heritage, wiggled excitedly at seeing me. I got down on the ground and left myself open for doggy kisses, of which there were many. Then she flung herself down on her back and I gently rubbed her tummy as her tongue lolled happily out the side of her mouth.

Linus smiled down at us. "We're doing all right, aren't we, Ivy? Getting our walk in before I head over to the library."

The explanation was unnecessary since I knew Linus's library routine down to a T. I stood back up and said, "Same here. Just exercising before heading over to work."

Linus said, "How is everything going for you? It's been very busy at the library lately, I've noticed."

"It definitely has. Of course, I like it that way. Not only does it make the day go by faster, it also means that people are making use of the library. And we've got some great volunteers that are helping with the shelving, so that makes everything a lot easier."

Linus said thoughtfully, "I believe I might have overheard Zelda a few times. She seems like a very focused volunteer."

I chuckled. "Let me guess—you heard Zelda telling off a patron for interrupting her while she was shelving. She doesn't appreciate questions when she's in her shelving zone. I've tried to get her to just redirect patrons to me, but she won't hear of it. She thinks the work I'm doing is far too important to answer questions about where books are. I've gotten so I have to keep an eye on her to make sure to intercept any patrons that are heading her way."

I reached down to rub Ivy again and her eyes closed happily.

Linus said hesitantly, "Thinking of the library and needing help . . . well, I can just ask you when you're at work. You're off right now." His face reddened.

I said, "Is there something you need some help with? Because that's my favorite part of working at the library. That's pretty much the main reason I became a librarian to begin with, aside from my love of books."

Linus brightened at the encouragement. He said slowly, "It's a different sort of problem—nothing to do with books or research."

"My job is to help with all sorts of problems."

Linus looked relieved. "It's a computer problem. I know you host those drop-ins, but I'm not totally sure I can wait until the next one to fix the issue. I can't remember my password for my banking. I usually set everything so that the computer remembers the logins for me, but this time, for some reason, it's not working. I don't know what to do to be able to access the banking site now."

I was glad to hear it was such a simple problem. I could help with most of the easier computer issues but for the harder ones I had to recruit my favorite high school student—Timothy, who knew just about everything there was to know about fixing any sort of tech problem. "I can help you with that. Is it a laptop?"

"A tablet," said Linus.

"Perfect. Just bring it in with you when you make it over to the library and we'll get you fixed up."

Linus looked vastly relieved and I wondered how long he'd been working or worrying about the login problem. "That's wonderful. Thank you."

I hesitated for a second. Thinking back to my conversation with Grayson last night, I wanted to invite Linus to come to my party. He wasn't really just a patron—he'd become something of a friend. The only problem was that Linus was even more introverted than I was and I didn't really want to put him on the spot. I said slowly, "I don't want you to feel any sort of pressure to come, but I'm having something of a get-together at my house before the football game on Saturday." I quickly added, "It's going to be one of those things where you can drop in and then drop back out again, if you like. Very casual. My house is so tiny that we'll be in my backyard and there'll be burgers and hotdogs and vegetarian options, too." I added the last because not only was I not sure whether Linus even ate meat, but I realized that I'd certainly need to invite vegan Luna to my party.

To my surprise, Linus didn't look as if he wanted to escape, which was his usual response when I invited him to do things like film club or a book club or other things at the library. Maybe it was because I'd emphasized the part about being able to just drop in and say hi and then leave again.

"That's very kind of you, Ann. I'd love to come for just a little while."

I beamed at him. "Great! That's really great, Linus. Um, let me write down the information for you." I had a small bag with me with my keys and license in it. Fortunately, (and somewhat inexplicably) there was also a small notepad and the stub of a pencil in there. I jotted down my address since he'd only briefly been by there once when he gave me a lift home after a particularly horrible date. And I came up with the time for the party on the spot. I handed him the piece of paper and said ruefully, "The get-together is so very casual that this is what passes for an invitation."

Linus carefully folded it and put it in his pocket. "Thank you. I'm looking forward to it. He looked down at his watch and said, "We'd both better be heading on if we're going to make it to the library when we're planning to. So good to see you, Ann."

Chapter Thirteen

I managed a fast walk and managed two miles in about thirty minutes. Then I had enough time to head back home, shower and dress, and pack up Fitz in his carrier to head over to work. As Linus and I had mentioned, it was already pretty crazy over there, but then, it was summer. A lot of folks liked coming into the library just to cool down when the days were hot. I had a hard time finding a place to park, which rarely happened.

I let Fitz out of his carrier behind the circulation desk so he had a little time to acclimate before anyone rushed up to pet him. But he didn't seem to need this time as he hopped out of the carrier, bounded around the desk, and trotted right over to a group of cooing teen girls. He looked as fetching as he could, which was mighty fetching indeed. They gently rubbed him and took numerous selfies with the orange and white cat.

Then I settled into working. I managed to finish up the library column for Grayson right before a patron came over to complain that we didn't have a copy of *Ulysses*.

I gave him a polite smile. "I can find it for you, if you like, unless it's checked out. Then I can put a hold on it for you."

The red-faced man said brusquely, "That would be pointless. You don't have it. I looked it up in the stacks, myself."

Retaining my polite tone I said, "Maybe it's misplaced in the stacks. We do have a copy—I've actually checked it out here, myself."

He shook his head, looking exceedingly annoyed. "It's simply not there. I went right over to the *W*s."

I paused. "The *W*s?"

"Yes. For Woolf," he said impatiently.

I diplomatically said, "You might be thinking of a different book. Maybe *Mrs. Dalloway*?"

He stared at me as if I'd lost my mind. A few more minutes of our conversation and he might just be right.

"I definitely was *not* looking for *Mrs. Dalloway*. I'd like to find *Ulysses* by Virginia Woolf."

I carefully answered, "That will be difficult to do. James Joyce wrote *Ulysses*."

He gave me a belligerent look. "Who on earth gave you a degree?"

I thought this was a rhetorical question at first, but he waited for an answer. "Whitby College," I finally said.

"Well, no wonder. They clearly didn't give you a good overview of classic lit or else you've forgotten everything you learned. Who's your manager?"

I glanced over at Wilson's glass-enclosed office. He raised his eyebrows at me as if recognizing my struggles and walked out to join us.

The red-faced patron saw Wilson walking in our direction in his suit and immediately left me to get better help as I emailed the library column I'd finished over to Grayson. When I wrapped that up, I saw that Wilson had taken the patron straight to James Joyce's *Ulysses*. The patron slunk over to self-checkout to avoid me and quietly slipped out the door. I hid a smile. Working with the public was, mostly, fantastic. I loved helping people out and connecting with folks who liked books, music, and films. The downside was the occasional tiresome person. But they always made for entertaining stories, later.

I put my head down and jumped back into the research project I was helping with, trying to get a stretch of work done quickly. The next time someone called my name, I looked up and saw Augusta Weber standing there.

"Hi there, Augusta. How are you doing?"

It was a fair question since Augusta looked completely stressed-out. There were lines of tension around her eyes and mouth and she looked like she might not have had a good night's sleep for a while.

She was holding a couple of books and gestured to them. "Well, I decided I wanted to take up a hobby as a way to relax. Fortunately, the library has plenty of resources for beginning knitters."

I smiled at her. "I've heard knitting is really relaxing. It's even something you can do at the same time as watching TV or listening to music."

Augusta nodded. "That's what I was hoping for. I want a distraction from everything that's happened with Jonas and Ted. Plus, I get really restless when I'm anxious and I figured this would be a good way for me to keep my hands busy."

"In case you're interested, there's a group of knitters that meets in the community room once a month," I suggested. "It might be a good way for you to get some tips and meet people, at the same time. They seem like a great group of women and are a range of different ages."

She seemed interested, so I looked up the information from the library calendar and jotted it down for her.

Augusta still hesitated by the desk and I had the feeling she wanted to talk a little but wasn't sure exactly how to jump in. I said, "So, how are you holding up? You mentioned needing a distraction. I know this has been a rough time for you."

She nodded and looked relieved at the cue to talk about it. "Burton has been asking a lot of questions. First about Jonas, of course. But then he started asking me about Ted—asking where I was when he died, trying to figure out how well I knew him."

I said, "That must be upsetting."

"And scary," Augusta quickly added. "I've never even gotten a traffic ticket before and now here I am with the police asking me about two murders? They must think I'm involved in both of them, Ann. I guess they think I got really upset with Jonas about him seeing someone else and killed him. I don't know why they think I had something to do with Ted Hill's death."

I shook my head and said, "Burton is just doing his job. Talking to everyone again is just how the process seems to work. I'm sure he's been speaking with everyone who's even tangentially involved with either Jonas or Ted."

This seemed to calm Augusta down just a little bit. "Okay. You're probably right. It just really startled me because I didn't even know Ted. I've always gotten my car serviced in Asheville when I'm in the area. I wouldn't even be able to pick Ted out of a line-up. The problem is that I don't have an alibi for either of those deaths, and I'm sure that doesn't look good. When Ted died, I was just at home watching romantic comedies. It's just not much of an alibi."

Linus walked by us on his way to the non-fiction section. He gave me a small smile and wave and kept on walking.

I smiled at her. "Well, most single people wouldn't have a great alibi. I know I wouldn't, not unless we could figure out a way to get Fitz to talk. Then he would recount the most boring evenings ever."

Fitz had decided to say hello to Augusta, leaping up onto the desk and brushing up against her. She rubbed him absently. "The thing that stinks is that now I have proof how bad I am at choosing romantic partners. I don't really know what I was thinking when I dated Jonas. I clearly remember realizing that our relationship was just not working. We spent a lot of time yelling at each other and I *still* dated him. I know there's got to be some good guys out there, but I have the worst taste in men."

"I think there are plenty of people who share that problem."

Augusta nodded. "I'm going to try and abstain from dating anybody for a while and see how that goes. My problem is that I'm trying to find my own completion in other people or re-lationships. I need to just focus on improving myself or trying new things. Like the knitting."

"That sounds really smart," I said.

Augusta said, "Well, I think it's time to do some soul-search-ing. Like I said, I see a pattern in the types of guys I've been going out with. But Jonas's death is a major wakeup call to me that I needed to get my act together. He was the kind of guy who made people mad. Somebody was angry enough with him to murder him in cold blood. What if I'd been in the house with him when he was killed?" She sighed. "I've been thinking a lot about Hattie. You know, the principal over at the high school?"

I nodded. "I know who she is."

"Yeah, I can't remember her last name right now. She and Jonas were involved, though, I think. At least, Jonas said they were, at some point. Maybe she got upset at being dumped and ended up taking that out on Jonas?" She shrugged. "I don't know—maybe it's a crazy idea. Jonas was supposed to have been seeing her before he started dating me. But I was thinking that she looks like the kind of person who's really self-contained and then blows it one day."

Augusta looked at her watch. "Oops, I've got to get going. I better do self-checkout real quick."

"I can get those for you," I said and checked out her craft books.

She gave me a smile. "See you later, Ann. And thanks." She headed for the door and stopped briefly as Linus returned from the non-fiction shelves. She gave him a cool greeting and kept on going.

I must have looked curious because Linus walked over. I smiled at him and said, "Excuse me for being nosy, but do you and Augusta know each other?"

It seemed a little unlikely to me, but Augusta's reaction had been so plain that I couldn't help but ask. Linus kept to himself for the most part and they were hardly contemporaries. But she definitely had seemed to recognize him and vice-versa.

Linus nodded. "She lives next door to me." He watched Augusta thoughtfully through the glass doors as she walked to her car in the parking lot. "I've only spoken with her a couple of times, so I'm surprised at her reaction just then. She seemed rather cool to me."

Knowing Linus, her reaction was making him worried. He was wondering if he'd done anything to bother her in any way. He corroborated this by saying slowly, "Ivy really isn't much of a barker. I don't think she's been irritating her or anything."

"Well, I know *you're* certainly quiet. And you spend a good deal of your time here at the library," I said.

He nodded, still looking a bit perturbed. "I've been a little concerned about Augusta, actually. Not that it's really any of my business. It's just that she's been acting very different lately from the way she ordinarily is. Naturally, she must have been very upset about her boyfriend's death." He added slowly, "I tend to notice people's routines. Maybe that's because I like following mine so closely every day."

This was the truth. Linus's schedule was pretty much written in stone. As a widower, it seemed he'd developed his schedule as a self-coping mechanism. He'd walk Ivy (who was still a sort of new addition to his routine), then head over to the library in his usual dress clothes. He'd start out with the newspapers and then move into fiction and non-fiction, take a break for lunch, and return to the library. If anyone adhered to a schedule, it was Linus.

"What kinds of things has she been doing?"

He said, "Leaving the house at different times. The fellow she was dating . . . the paper called him Jonas."

There was a slight question in his tone and I nodded.

Linus hesitated and then said, "It's just that he didn't seem like the right person for her. Actually, he didn't seem like the right person for *anyone*."

"From what I understood, he was a very difficult person to be around."

Linus nodded in confirmation. "Whenever I saw him, he sounded cruel. I never heard him say a kind thing to Augusta. Often, she wouldn't even let him in her house, which was how I ended up hearing some of their confrontations." He pinkened a bit. "I spend a good deal of time on my screened porch with a collection of plants. I'm afraid this all makes me sound very nosy."

"Not at all," I said firmly. "This information might even prove to be useful for the investigation."

Linus nodded again, looking resigned. "Yes. I've been thinking that for the last twenty-four hours. I didn't realize who Jonas was until the paper printed a photo of him in yesterday's edition. The previous news stories didn't have any pictures of him. But of course I'll share this information with Burton."

"How did Augusta react during these arguments? Or was it mostly a one-sided thing?"

"It definitely wasn't one-sided. I think Augusta probably gave as good as she got during the arguments. It was never physical or I'd have called the police right then, of course. But their relationship seemed anything but healthy. Augusta seemed very high-strung and was understandably very upset after their altercations. I kept wondering why she didn't end their involvement. Of course, it wasn't any of my business." He shook his head.

"And Jonas would come over at unusual times. Sometimes very late at night. Ivy would hear his car and trot over to the window to see what was going on."

Then Linus, always keen to keep to his routine, glanced at his watch. "I should probably let you go now, Ann."

"Enjoy your reading," I said.

The pace at the library picked up again and I spent the next hour or so completely swamped. Then things abruptly changed and it was quiet again. Zelda stomped into the library, looking grim, as always.

"Everything okay with the car?" I asked her.

She gave me a thumbs-up. "Runs like a dream."

I had the feeling that the elderly sedan had likely not run like a dream even in its infancy. But I gave her a return thumbs-up which she didn't even see because she was so focused on getting started with her shelving.

I was updating the library's social media accounts with upcoming activities when Luna walked over, looking stressed. And stress and Luna were not usually acquainted with each other.

"I'm getting ready to pull my hair out." She made a face. "Or maybe I'm getting ready to pull *Wilson's* hair out."

I gave her a sympathetic look. "I'm sorry. It's been so busy here today that I didn't even notice if Mona had come by."

Luna nodded. "Mom had me drive her over during my lunch break because Wilson has been avoiding her calls."

"Avoiding her *calls*?" Wilson was, usually, so much of a gentleman that I had a hard time taking this in.

"Well, okay, not really *avoiding* them. At least not all the time. He definitely screened out a couple of her calls and then told her later that his phone was acting up. But whenever he answers the phone, he has this really clipped, five-minute conversation with her where it's totally obvious he's trying to get off the phone as fast as he can."

I asked, "How was he today when Mona came over?"

Luna put her hands on her hips. "He made Mom cry. Not in front of him, but as soon as she left his office, she burst into tears and I had to drive her home."

I was about to tell her I was sorry again when a grating voice croaked, "What? That nice lady?"

It was Zelda, walking by with her cart. Her eyebrows knit together. I was surprised that Zelda would even have registered who Mona was. Zelda was one to just keep her head down and plow through all her work.

Luna said, "That's right. I think I saw Mom talking to you last week."

Zelda said gruffly, "She brought in some doughnuts and there were some left over in the breakroom. She told me to take them home." She glowered in the direction of Wilson's office. "He's dating her, isn't he?"

Luna said, "They've been going out together but Wilson has been acting pretty cold lately. He's worried about something and it's affecting his relationship with Mom."

Zelda's eyes narrowed. "It shouldn't."

Luna chuckled at Zelda's ferocity. "You're right. But it is. He doesn't want to involve her in the thing that's worrying him. And we can't say anything because we work for him." She glanced across the room. She lowered her voice just a little and continued, "And we should probably talk about this another time because he's heading over."

I recognized the combative look in Zelda's eyes. I'd seen it before at homeowner association meetings when a homeowner thought they could add a ten-foot fence to their property or paint their house lavender.

Zelda muttered, "I do *not* work for him. I'm a volunteer."

Wilson joined us and said, "Ann, I was wondering if you could take a look at the library calendar and see if there's room to schedule more programming."

"*More* programming?" I frowned. "I was just looking at the calendar a few minutes ago while I updated our social media. I've gotten the impression that the staff looked stretched thin for the upcoming month. There has been a lot of patron volume in the library and the program calendar is pretty full, too."

"Maybe room for a tech event, then? Just one additional program. Perhaps it could even be streamed."

I recognized this particular mood of Wilson's. He didn't react to stress very well, as evident from his complete disconnection from Mona. When he was stressed out and felt as if his life was out of his control, his favorite way of dealing with it was to add things into his life that he *could* control. In this case, library programming.

Still, that didn't mean that utter chaos in the library needed to ensue. I was about to explore the idea with him that dragging staff away from helping patrons to man additional library events might not be a good idea when Wilson moved on to another topic.

He gave Luna a vague look. "Is Mona not at the library? I thought I saw her earlier, but she doesn't seem to be here now."

Luna looked as if she could write a doctorate thesis on the subject but managed to say, "No, I needed to take her back home."

Wilson gave a stiff nod of his head.

Zelda, however, didn't seem to want to let the topic rest. She tilted her henna-dyed head to one side and regarded Wilson through narrowed eyes. In her cigarette-ruined voice she said, "I hear Mona's feelings were hurt."

Wilson's face creased into a frown as he looked at Zelda in surprise. "Sorry?"

This was pure, unadulterated Zelda. This was the way she was in attack mode at HOA meetings. "That Mona is a nice lady. She's even sent me home with food she baked before. Makes me a little upset that you've made her feel bad."

Wilson now looked extremely uncomfortable. Zelda's hands were on her hips and her thin lips were set into an uncompromising line. Luna looked admiringly at Zelda. And I was trying very hard not to smile.

Wilson said gruffly, "I'm simply trying to keep Mona from getting involved in a stressful situation that she shouldn't have to deal with."

Zelda snorted. "Mona sure looks like an adult to me. She should have the chance to decide whether your situation is something she wants to get involved with or not. You gotta give her a chance."

Wilson looked very much as if he wished he had a comeback for this remark. However, volunteers were like gold in the library—we never wanted to make one upset. Wilson always carefully respected the feelings of both volunteers and library trustees. Both groups were vital, in their own way.

So he said diplomatically, "That's good advice, Zelda. I will have to mull that over. Right now." And with that, he swiftly walked back to his office with Fitz padding along behind him.

Zelda, mission accomplished, gave a bob of her head and trundled her cart over to the nonfiction area.

Chapter Fourteen

Luna gave a low whistle. "Wow, she really can pack a punch, can't she? I thought she always just kept her head down and shelved books the whole time. I had no idea that she even knew who Mom was."

"Mona is so friendly and outgoing that I bet she reached out to Zelda first. Besides, she apparently gave Zelda food. And you know how good a cook your mother is," I said. "Zelda is always one to take on a project. I guess she saw the opportunity and pounced on it."

Luna said, "Well, maybe it will do some good. I hate to see Mom retreat inward again . . . and she was doing so well hanging out here at the library and dating Wilson."

"Let's keep our fingers crossed that it works."

"Uh-oh. Wilson is coming this way." Luna froze, uncertain whether she wanted to scamper over to the children's area or speed hijack the book cart from Zelda just to immediately have something to do.

Wilson, however, didn't look as if he was planning on fussing about our chatting. He had a furrow between his brows and seemed to be somewhat at a loss for words. He finally said, "Luna, is your mom still around?"

Luna nodded. "I think she's just hanging out in the periodical section."

Wilson cleared his throat. "Could you and your mom join me in my office for a few minutes? Ann, you too. Get someone to cover the desk for you."

"Sure," said Luna and I, sounding like a bemused Greek chorus.

A few minutes later, we were all sitting in Wilson's office and watching as he hemmed and hawed for a few moments. Wilson looked pained. He appeared to be thinking through the exact phrasing of what he wanted to say. Then he shook his head. "I may as well tell you everything. I've been keeping secrets for too long and they're making me miserable. But if you can, please keep this to yourself."

Luna's eyes were wide and Mona blurted, "Of course we will. Please tell us what's going on."

Wilson hesitated, stalling by petting Fitz, who'd bounded in after us as we'd entered the office. "I just don't want to have you all think differently about me."

I said, "Wilson, we've known you for a while. We're not going to change our opinion about you."

Wilson nodded and cleared his throat. "The man who was killed, Jonas Merchant, was blackmailing me."

Mona and Luna stared at Wilson in disbelief. "Blackmailing *you*?"

I couldn't blame them for being shocked. I couldn't possibly imagine what Wilson could have done for anyone to blackmail him. Failed to return a phone call? Had an overdue library book at his home for several weeks? Wilson had always seemed a major rule-follower in every way.

Wilson flushed a little and stared down at his carefully-clipped nails. "I'm afraid he did. You see, I was a different person years ago. You know that I'm a teetotaler now."

Actually, I didn't, but that's because I didn't really socialize with my boss. I nodded, though, as did Luna and Mona.

"Well, there was an incident several years ago that precipitated that decision. I'd had a few drinks at a bar and decided I should walk home."

Luna said, "Well, that part sounds above reproach."

Wilson took a deep breath. "It gets worse. I was very unsteady on my feet and jostled a table on my way out of the bar. The . . . gentleman . . . who was sitting at the table ended up covered with beer. Apparently, he wasn't the most forgiving of men. He started slugging me and I hit back in self-defense." He let out a big sigh. "Burton's predecessor on the force arrived and charged me with public drunkenness and disorderly conduct."

Mona burst out laughing and Wilson looked at her in surprise. "Goodness, Wilson! A bar fight. And here I was thinking you'd killed someone or had a DUI or something."

Wilson glanced anxiously at all of us but relaxed at our expressions. "Well, I can promise you it's something that's caused me a lot of grief. The individual I fought with didn't know me and no one else aside from bartender was in there. I suppose the bartender must be accustomed to keeping secrets. I was so relieved that no one knew about my arrest. Then and there, I decided that alcohol and I weren't a good fit for each other. I don't like making poor decisions."

"That was smart of you," I said.

Wilson said dryly, "It was good that I finally made some sort of rational decision."

Luna said, "So . . . you mentioned blackmail. Jonas somehow knew what had happened? Why would he wait so long to blackmail you, if he did? You don't mean that he's been extorting money from you for years?"

"No. When I was being escorted by the police from the bar, Jonas's father happened to be driving past. Apparently, Mr. Merchant told his son everything during their phone conversations. And Mr. Merchant was very partial to local gossip. He knew just about everything that happened in Whitby and passed it along."

Mona frowned. "He knew his son was planning on blackmailing people with the information? That seems like a very weird father and son relationship."

"No, Mr. Merchant didn't know about Jonas's activities. At least, not according to Jonas. Mr. Merchant was simply a garrulous old soul who liked to keep his finger on the pulse of the town and spread gossip. But Jonas decided to take advantage of the gossip he'd gleaned from his father once he'd moved here. I suppose Jonas might not even have tried blackmailing anyone until his father died."

"It was a money-making opportunity for him," said Luna indignantly. "While he ruined people's lives."

Wilson nodded. "Exactly."

"But he did have a regular job?" asked Mona.

Wilson said, "He worked at some sort of office downtown. But either it wasn't making him the money he thought he needed, or he doesn't make very much at all. At any rate, he was clearly supplementing his income with blackmail."

"When did he first get in touch with you?"

"It was a few months ago," said Wilson with a sigh. "Maybe I shouldn't have cared so much, but I did. I care about my position in town and what people who live here think of me."

"Of course you do," I murmured.

Encouraged by this, Wilson went on. "Maybe it's silly or prideful, but it's a small town and I've spent a good deal of time trying to create a decent reputation for myself. When Jonas got in touch with me, I felt completely sick. I worried about what the board of trustees at the library would think. I wondered if it might hurt my relationship with you, Mona, because I'd been too ashamed to mention that I had an arrest in my past."

"As if that would matter to me," said Mona.

"So you paid him?" asked Luna.

Wilson shook his head. "I knew that blackmail would never end. I'd be paying out to Jonas for years and years if I started down that particular road. I couldn't stand the thought of being beholden to anyone else. Besides, I just don't have that sort of money. I ended up calling him and trying to appeal to his better self."

"Did that work?" I asked.

Wilson absently rubbed Fitz. "He didn't seem to *have* a better self. Besides, he said he'd take great pleasure in taking me down. That I thought I was more respectable than anyone else and I should be proved wrong."

Mona asked, "What did you do?"

Wilson said, "I just didn't pay. Jonas had been sending me threatening notes and part of me thought about taking them to Burton for evidence. But then I realized they were typed on computer paper and it would probably be my word against his. The morning I found Jonas dead, I was at his house to try to convince him in person to stop trying to blackmail me."

"And you found his body, instead," said Luna. "Part of you must have been relieved."

"Not a bit," said Wilson sadly. "After all, I became a suspect." He gave Mona a pleading look. "I'm so sorry I've been pushing you away. I just didn't want you to get mixed up in all this. Believe me, I had nothing to do with Jonas's death."

"Of course you didn't," said Mona stoutly, reaching over to give Wilson a hug.

Luna said, "Have you told Burton about this? Just let him know why you were over at Jonas's house that morning?"

I was wondering the same thing. He sure hadn't wanted to divulge the information when he'd first spoken with Burton. Had he filled him in?

Wilson took off his glasses and rubbed his eyes wearily. "I didn't have to. Eventually, he found notes in Jonas's house outlining what he was blackmailing me for. Unfortunately, it made me look even more guilty that I hadn't disclosed it earlier." He turned to Mona again. "I'm really a different person now than I was. I'm embarrassed to admit, but I've always been uptight. I discovered about a decade or so ago that alcohol was a way for me to unwind. Now I know, of course, that it wasn't good for me at all. It might be fine for other people," he added quickly. "For me, though, it was basically poison. It made me act in ways I wouldn't ordinarily. I was so ashamed of my behavior. The charges were reduced, but I was so worried everyone in town would know. And you know how I feel about our trustees."

I did. Wilson would do anything for our library trustees. The last thing he would want to do was create some sort of a scandal that they'd end up gossiping about.

"I kept waiting for it to be the talk of the town. I was so very grateful to find that Worth, Jonas's father, never said anything, nor did the police chief who was serving then."

Mona said fervently, "Well, *I'm* grateful that you finally told us what's been going on. We've all been worried about you."

Luna added, "I'm sure Burton doesn't seriously consider you a suspect. You're . . . Wilson."

He gave her a wry smile. "Let's hope you're right."

Luna and I walked out of Wilson's office, leaving Mona and Wilson together to talk things out.

"I have to say that was, by far, the most exciting library meeting I've ever been a part of," said Luna. "Wow. I mean, Wilson is such a straight arrow that it's hard to even imagine he would ever break the law. I felt bad for him when he was telling us—he looked so ashamed of himself. But good for him for going completely off alcohol."

I nodded. "He's got so much self-discipline that it probably really helped. I know he's relieved that your mom took it so well."

I paused. "On sort of a different subject, I'm actually hosting a get-together on Saturday. Do you think your mom and Wilson would be interested in coming by? I thought I'd feel you about it first."

"Whoa, whoa, whoa. Let's just backup a minute there. You're *hosting* a *get-together*?" Luna's eyes were wide.

"Hey, I'm not *that* introverted."

Luna said, "Well, I've never heard of you hosting anything before. This is a red-letter day. What made you decide to host it?"

I shrugged. "I thought maybe a barbeque before the football game would be nice."

Luna put her hands on her hips and gave me a sideways look. "Okay, what happened to the real Ann Beckett and who is this imposter?"

I chuckled. "All right. I just thought that having something casual at my house before an event that everyone would want to get back to their homes for sounded like a good idea. The fact of the matter is that I'm trying to be a little more outgoing because of Grayson."

"Grayson, who is *very* outgoing."

"Right," I said. "I'm definitely not going to try and compete with Grayson's extroversion. But he's invited me to a few events lately and I've turned him down flat. He seemed fine with it, but I kept thinking that he was the one doing all the adjusting and I was the one who wasn't really trying. So I figured I'd try to host something on my home turf."

Luna nodded. "Home team advantage. Very smart. Who's coming to this barbeque?"

"So far, I'd only asked Grayson to invite his friends over. I was supposed to meet them at one of the events I turned down.

I invited Linus, too, and I was shocked that he accepted. I figured it might make me a little less nervous about the party if I invited a bunch of people I know."

Luna said, "I think it's a good idea for you to populate the party with people you know. It might make things easier. As far as inviting Mom and Wilson, I think Mom would love it. She's been a lot more active now that she and Wilson are going out."

"Do you think Burton could come? And you're obviously invited, too."

Luna looked doubtful. "*Maybe* he could come? But he seems pretty slammed with the case—I haven't been able to see much of him at all. I'm sure he would probably appreciate the invitation, though."

"How are things going with the two of you?" I asked curiously.

"Oh, pretty well. We have a low-key relationship, which is sort of the way I want it. I do have the feeling that Burton would like more than that, but he's also happy to keep things moving slowly. I just had so many bad relationships in the past that I guess I'm not in any hurry to get seriously involved."

I was about to respond to this when Zelda, passing by with her cart again, gave a peremptory cough at our continued conversation. Luna gave a giggle and we scattered quickly.

Saturday came up before I knew it. Or maybe time just flies when you're a little nervous. I picked up the hotdogs and burgers at the store and then turned a critical eye on my house and yard to see how it might look to someone who hadn't seen it before.

"Don't clean up, please," Grayson told me when I was casually wiping down the top of my refrigerator as if it was something I did all the time. "Everything always looks neat and tidy here."

"Except, perhaps, the top of my fridge." I showed him the offending paper towel of grime and made a face.

"No one in this group is tall enough to see the top of your fridge," he insisted. "Your house is a warm, comfortable, cozy place. There are books scattered everywhere, music is always playing in the background. And your yard is incredible. Everyone is going to love being here."

I wasn't sure about that, but I was happy to try and believe him.

I stopped cleaning the top of the fridge and dismounted the small step-stool I'd pulled out to help with the chore. Then I turned my critical gaze to my baseboards.

Grayson said, "Ann, stop. I'm serious. Just relax. You're going to have a houseful of people over here in about four hours. That's probably going to stress you out on some level, especially with meeting new people and trying to make sure old friends are having a good time. Use this time to just hang out—put your feet up, hydrate, play with Fitz. Everyone is going to have a good time and they're not going to be going through your house with a checklist to see how clean your baseboards are."

I glanced over at the offending baseboards again and saw that, actually, they were pretty clean. I said, "You're right. You can tell I'm just an inexperienced hostess."

Grayson reached out and gave me a hug. "You're a great hostess. And girlfriend. I appreciate this so much."

And suddenly, with Grayson's arms around me, I *did* relax.

I even took Grayson's advice. I curled up on the sofa with Fitz, my book, and some jazz music and had some quiet time to myself before everyone started coming over.

About half an hour before the guests were due to arrive, Grayson came back over and set up some chairs he'd brought over so that we'd have more outdoor seating. We turned the pre-game show on and kept it on mute, turning on the captions. I started a music playlist that had a variety of different songs on it and tinkered with the volume to get it right.

Luck was on my side with the weather. After a couple of disastrous-sounding forecasts, something had changed with the jet stream and we now had bright sun, a few wispy cotton-candy clouds, and a lovely light breeze.

Then people started trickling in. To my surprise, the first to arrive was Burton.

"Hi there," I said, pleased. "I wasn't sure you were going to be able to make it."

He grinned at me. "Luna said this was a momentous occasion, so I thought I'd just stick my head in for a few minutes, at least. Maybe I need to take some pictures to memorialize the event."

I gave him a rueful look. "Luna was right, ha. This may be my first and last party-hosting experiment."

Burton chuckled. "Well, everything looks and smells amazing." He gestured over to the grill, where Grayson had just thrown a few burgers on a plate.

"Want a burger while you're here?" asked Grayson.

"Somebody's got to be the first one to eat at a party," I said when I noticed he was looking a bit undecided.

"Might as well be me, then," he said. He started putting fixings on the burger and bun. He turned to me and asked, "Any more developments regarding things you might have heard? I figured while I was here, I should check in with you and see what you might have found out."

I sighed. "I'm not really sure what I've really learned. I know Hattie Gray thought Ted might know something. I'm guessing that something was what led to his death. Have you found out what it was?"

Burton shook his head regretfully. "Now I wish I'd pressed Ted further when he was alive. Or that he'd been a little more open with me."

I said, "Maybe he wasn't sure about what he'd seen or heard. He was probably worried about getting someone in trouble with the police, especially if there was a chance they could be innocent. He could have wanted to speak with them in private to make sure he understood what he'd seen."

"Which was the nail in his coffin," said Burton somberly. "I wish he'd confided to me instead and let me figure out if what he saw was significant or not. The person he approached must immediately have considered him a threat. Anything else?"

I thought about Reggie and Flora's burgeoning relationship but knew that was more like gossip and less like the type of information Burton was looking for. I wondered if Flora was going to be able to make it to the party. She'd definitely not been acting like herself lately, which I figured could be attributed to the fact that she was busy with the house and settling Jonas's affairs. "Flora reiterated that she had nothing to do with her brother's death, despite getting the house. To be honest, I can't picture Flora involved in all this. She's just such a gentle person and spends most of her time with plants."

Burton smiled and nodded, but didn't exactly jump in to defend Flora. I supposed there had been plenty of times in his law enforcement career that suspects had surprised him.

Burton nodded. "Of course, it's only natural for her to say that she didn't really care that much about getting the house. From what I've been able to tell, she's putting a lot of time, attention, and love into getting the house and the yard back into shape."

"I think she's really going to love having a yard of her own," I said. "As a renter, that's something she's really missed. And she works at a plant nursery! It must be like working at an animal shelter when you know you can't take a dog or cat home."

Burton nodded and I could tell he thought that getting a house made for a natural motive. He said, "And then we have the professor next door. The neighbor who had to put up with all Jonas's bad behavior." He sighed. "Nobody was a fan of Jonas's and that doesn't really help me out. I was sure Ted was behind it all."

"Yeah," I said. "It's unfortunate that Ted didn't just immediately reach out to you to let you know what he knew. But he seemed like the kind of guy who would want to be sure about something before he said it. He wasn't the sort of person who liked making mistakes, especially the kind of mistake that might send someone to jail."

Burton took a morose bite of his burger, nodding thoughtfully. He swallowed and then said, "Then we have your library friend, Hattie."

"Yes. She's obviously been very upset about everything that's happened."

Burton said, "Is she more upset about being a suspect in the investigation? Or at the deaths of the two victims?"

"Naturally, she's upset at Ted's death. I'm sure Jonas's must have been a huge relief to her. But now she's upset at something else—she's feeling guilty at suspecting Ted. Apparently, she feels like her remaining time with Ted was tainted because she felt sure he must have something to do with Jonas's death. Ted did have plenty of motive—both his sister and Hattie were being blackmailed by Jonas. He told Hattie he didn't have anything to do with it, but she had a tough time believing him. Now that he's gone, she really regrets doubting him."

Burton said, "Well, he did really have a good motive. I'm not surprised that she was worried he was involved in Jonas's death. Anybody else?"

"I talked to Augusta again recently. She's trying to work through her stress by picking up a new hobby."

"Was it our police investigation that was making her so stressed out? Or do you think she's actually missing Jonas?"

I said, "I got the impression that it was a combination of things. Definitely the fact that she's considered a suspect, but also Jonas's death. She said that she didn't know Ted, though, so she doesn't seem directly affected by his passing." I shrugged. "She said that Jonas had told her that he'd had a relationship with Hattie at some point."

Burton's heavy eyebrows lifted. "Did she, now? Well, that sounds like a complete fabrication. But was it Jonas's fabrication? Or was it Augusta's?"

"You think Augusta might lie about something like that?"

"Absolutely," said Burton. "She might have said that to deflect from the truth. Maybe she *did* kill Jonas when she lost control with him after finding out he was cheating on her. By telling you that Jonas was dating Hattie, she's providing a red herring for us to investigate. I haven't heard anything about Jonas's involvement with Hattie aside from the fact that he was blackmailing her."

"Or, I suppose Jonas might have lied to Augusta about having dated Hattie," I said slowly.

Burton nodded. "Exactly. Maybe Augusta saw Jonas and Hattie having a really animated conversation together or meeting together somewhere. Augusta apparently wasn't initially aware of his blackmailing activities. Instead of telling her that he knew Hattie because he was trying to extort money from her, he might have told her that Hattie was an ex of his."

"Makes sense," I said. "Or maybe Augusta is simply misremembering."

Burton finished his burger and looked at his watch. He said regretfully, "Sorry, but I've really got to run."

"Hey, I just appreciate that you took the time to come by at all."

Burton said, "Tell Luna I said hi when she comes by. Looks like she's running a little late."

"No surprise there," I said with a chuckle. "Punctuality has never been Luna's forte. But she has a lot of other good qualities."

Burton gave a wistful look. "Yes, she sure does. Okay, see you soon."

Chapter Fifteen

I watched him go. He looked like he had the weight of the world on his shoulders. I was sure that trying to solve these murders was a real burden. Whitby was a small town and the residents weren't going to be very receptive to having a killer in their midst. I also wondered if part of his worries were related to Luna. From what she'd told me, Burton was a lot more invested in their relationship than she was. I wondered if that was just because she hadn't fallen as hard for him as he had for her, or whether it was because her other relationships had soured her against men, in general.

More guests were filing into the backyard, carrying a variety of different side dishes. No matter what, we were definitely going to have enough food, despite the number of people I'd invited over. I'd sent an invite to a few of my neighbors (most of whom had also known my great-aunt who lived here before me), my library coworkers, and Grayson's friends. I felt positive that I'd stacked the deck with enough people I was well-acquainted with to be able to feel confident enough to also meet the people who were important to Grayson.

I saw a boyish-looking man in his thirties come in with what appeared to be chicken wings on a platter . . . and Augusta Weber, who gave me a quick wave and a wry look. I'd emailed the invites and put my phone number on there for folks to text me their RSVPs. Jeremy had asked if he could bring a date with him and I'd said yes, so I was able to narrow down which of Grayson's friends this was. I was definitely a little surprised to see the date was Augusta, considering she'd just told me she was going to try to take a break from dating and focus on herself. I'd gotten the impression from talking with Augusta that she was going to take a break from dating for a while and focus on self-development and crafts. She'd specifically mentioned that she had a habit of going for the wrong kind of guy. But maybe, when she met Jeremy, she had the feeling that he could really be the one for her. I hoped it worked out well for her.

Grayson saw my expression and misinterpreted it. "Sorry, I thought Jeremy asked you if it was all right for him to bring a guest."

"No, he definitely did. I was just surprised at his choice of guest, that's all."

Grayson looked closer and said, "Wow, it's Augusta. Jeremy didn't tell me who he was bringing with him."

Jeremy strode over to Grayson and they hugged in a clapping-noisily-on-the-back sort of way. I walked over to introduce myself and say hi to Augusta as Grayson was pulled away by a neighbor who'd just arrived.

"Hi, I'm Jeremy," the man said, dimples punctuating his cheeks as he grinned at me. "And you must be Ann. I've heard a ton of good things about you from Grayson."

I reached out to shake hands but he pulled me in for a quick hug. "Good to see you again, Ann! Thanks for having us all over."

Augusta gave me a shy look. "Hi, Ann. I hope this is okay."

"Absolutely," I said with a smile. "I'm really glad you could make it."

Jeremy said, "Great place you have here, Ann."

Augusta nodded. "The house *and* the yard. You must really have a green thumb with all the shrubs and flowers you have here."

I chuckled. "Well, I wish I could claim that, but it's categorically untrue. This was my great-aunt's house and *she* was the one with the green thumb. I have more of a caretaker role here and just have to worry about the upkeep. So I weed, throw fertilizer out, and water."

Jeremy glanced behind me and said, "Looks like the whole gang's here."

Sure enough, there was a tall, thin man with a goatee coming in with a big guy who was giving some sort of sports stats in a loud voice. Grayson walked over to greet them and Jeremy joined them, too.

I turned back to Augusta with a smile. "There are burgers over there on the table with all of the fixings. Or, if you'd like, I made a big salad."

Augusta glanced over at the table and nodded. "Thanks. I think I might string out the eating over the course of the party. Just because it gives me something to do, you know."

I chuckled. "Having been on plenty of dates, I *do* know what you're talking about. Sometimes there are awkward silences and you can fill them by asking Jeremy to get you some chips or some salad or a drink or something."

"Actually, a drink is sounding pretty good right now," said Augusta, looking back over at the table. "You must think this is all kind of sudden. After all, I was just telling you that I was planning on sticking with knitting and self-improvement instead of going out on dates."

I said lightly, "I just figured you must have found a good prospect and decided to give dating a go again. There's nothing wrong with that."

Augusta nodded. "Yeah, that's exactly what happened."

"Is this a first date for you two?"

"It is. I think Jeremy was thinking it might be easier with a bunch of people around. I was nervous about coming until I found out you were the one who was hosting. I figured at least I'd know one person here and I wouldn't have to stick to Jeremy like a limpet."

I wondered if this type of date really *was* easier. It seemed to me like going on a quick coffee made a lot more sense, but I was hardly the dating expert, despite the number of awful first dates I'd gone on through the years.

Augusta's gaze followed Jeremy, who was still catching up with the other guys. "He seems pretty nice so far. Anyway, he's easy to hang out with and, after Jonas, that's the sort of person I was looking for."

"I'm imagining that Jonas was *not* easy to hang out with."

Augusta snorted. "There was really no hanging out with Jonas. He was so intense. Plus, I never really knew what he was thinking. Considering how much blackmailing and stuff he was doing, I suppose that's a good thing. So far, Jeremy seems like an open book in comparison." She squared her shoulders. "Okay, well, I'm going ahead and making myself something small and then I'll meet his other friends."

"If you need to be thrown a life preserver, just let me know," I said with a smile. "Been there, done that. I can always butt into a conversation and start spouting some arcane library stuff."

She smiled back at me. "Thanks."

Jeremy came back over to join us and I paused instead of leaving the two of them together. Augusta definitely seemed nervous and looked relieved to have me around. She also was being uncharacteristically quiet and didn't seem eager to take the conversational reins. Trying to be a good hostess, I jumped in, instead.

"Jeremy, have you lived here in Whitby long?" I asked politely. Since I'd been here most of my life, if I didn't know someone in town, it was because they'd moved in within the last five years or so. Although it was a small town, the lake and the mountains nearby were a big draw.

"Just a few years," he said in his easy manner. "My folks live about an hour away, so I moved here to be a little closer to them and also have access to all the different outdoor activities. I love hiking and kayaking and all that kind of stuff."

Augusta furrowed her brow. She didn't strike me as an outdoorsy person. Hopefully, there were plenty of other things that they had in common.

We chatted for a couple of minutes, to Augusta's relief, but I could see a bunch of other people coming into the yard who I needed to greet. I said, "Thanks for bringing the chicken in, Jeremy. Please go ahead and help your plates with whatever you'd like and find a spot to sit. We're going to be really casual today."

"Thanks, Ann," said Augusta, looking toward one of the tables where the food was laid out. I also had several card tables set up for extra seating around the yard since I didn't want anyone to feel like they had to stand and eat.

Grayson joined us again and said, "Lots of food over there. I'm about to fix myself a plate, too."

Jeremy said, "Whatever you did to the burgers smells awesome, Grayson. But you've always been the cook of the group." He turned to me and smiled. "Hey, you should come to my place next weekend. I'm having some people over just to hang out for a little while."

Grayson winked at me and said, "Thanks, Jeremy. Ann and I will take a look at our calendars and let you know."

I gave Grayson a relieved look. Fun as this was, and I *was* enjoying myself more than I thought I would, I wasn't sure if this was something I wanted to do every weekend.

Grayson gently put an arm around me. "Plus, there was that exhibit you and I were thinking about going to."

Jeremy chuckled. "There you go again, having to prove yourself as the most cultured member of the group. No pressure—you don't even have to let me know in advance because it's *that* casual. Drop in, even for a few minutes, if you have the time."

One of the other guys dropped Jeremy's name in conversation and he turned to plunge into whatever football-related discussion was going on there.

I chuckled. "Thanks, Grayson. I think I need to practice my saying-no skills."

He smiled at me. "I have a feeling that being a librarian doesn't help with that. You're practically programmed to always be helpful and give things a try." He glanced across the yard and said, "Looks like Wilson made it."

I turned to follow his gaze and saw Wilson there, looking a little awkward at being out of his usual habitat. He was wearing his version of casual clothing—khaki pants and a button-down shirt with the cuffs slightly, and very-precisely, rolled-up.

We walked over to him. "Hi, Wilson," I said with a smile. "Glad you could make it."

Wilson gave us a tight smile in return. I guessed he was still feeling awkward about telling us about his long-ago arrest. "Thanks for inviting me. I'm sorry it took so long for me to respond."

"You're fine," I said. "This is one of those really laid-back get-togethers."

Grayson gave me a wry smile. It was a get-together that was laid-back for the *attendees*, perhaps, but not necessarily for the hostess.

Grayson gestured over to the grill. "We've got some burgers and hot dogs ready. Or vegetables and salad, if you'd like it. Can I get you a plate?"

Wilson turned to Grayson and said, "A burger would be great, thanks. They smell wonderful."

Grayson put a patty on a plate and Wilson started putting condiments and fixings on it. "Is Mona here yet?"

"Not yet," I said. But then we both heard Luna's voice, which tended to carry. It was a good thing that libraries had turned into places where noise was completely acceptable because I could often hear Luna's distinctive voice wafting from the children's department.

Luna walked ~~out~~ into the backyard. She looked somewhat blinding as she was wearing neon colors from head to toe. I had the feeling that because Luna tried to be somewhat conservative with her attire at work, she went a little crazy with it in her off-hours since it had been repressed all day.

Luna spotted me with Wilson right away and came over. Her mother was with her, but Mona wore a more-traditional outfit with flowing slacks and a jaunty top. She spotted Wilson and beamed at him, hurrying over. I was glad to see Wilson relax a little and even smile back at her.

I greeted a couple of neighbors who had come by, including Zelda. Zelda was giving a suspicious glare at the surrounding guests. And I saw one of our mutual neighbors carefully hiding from Zelda behind a flowering bush. I seemed to recall something about him having a commercial vehicle parked on his property, which was in violation of the homeowner association agreement. I decided that I might have to bring the poor man a plate of food if he ended up stuck behind the bush much longer.

Instead, he was able to quickly escape as Zelda came over to speak with me. She gave me a grim look and I fully expected her to tell me that I'd left my trash bin out on the street too long before rolling it back to the house after a late shift at the library. But instead she barked, "Good party. Thank you for inviting me."

That was the thing about Zelda. You could never tell from her expression what she was planning on saying.

"Oh, it's my pleasure. I'm just glad you could make it. There are burgers on the table or a big salad, if you'd rather eat vegan."

Zelda wrinkled up her brow. "Eat what?"

"Um, vegan? I mean, if you'd rather just have vegetables."

Zelda gazed at me as if this was the most remarkable and bizarre idea she'd ever heard. "Burger's fine." She pursed her lips. "I might need a cigarette, though."

"I'm afraid I don't have any," I said, before realizing that she was pulling one out from her purse. "Oh, you mean that you might need to *smoke* one."

Zelda lifted an etched-on eyebrow. "Is it okay to smoke one outside here?"

The only problem was that my backyard was becoming quickly filled up. "Maybe we should just stand over here in the corner for a minute or two," I said. I figured it would be more diplomatic if I escorted her over to the corner so she wouldn't feel as if she was in some sort of time-out.

She quirked the other brow at me and we walked over to the quiet corner of the yard.

Frankly, I had no idea how long it took for someone to smoke a cigarette. I thought perhaps, with dedicated and focused puffing, a cigarette could be consumed in about three minutes. Unfortunately, Zelda seemed to be in no hurry and, in fact, appeared to be interested in conversation. Conversation that decidedly extended the length of time we were standing in the corner.

She held the cigarette in one hand, seeming to enjoy just holding it and letting ash accumulate as she looked around the backyard with narrowed eyes. I saw my other neighbor carefully slip inside my house in response.

"How is the new job going?" I asked her.

This unleashed the aforementioned conversation. "Busy place," she said with a grunt. "They've caught up at the garage, though. Still, tons of people coming in with broken cars and trucks."

"I'm sure you have the place running smoothly now," I said cheerfully.

She raised her eyebrow again. "Oh, I do. Everything is ship-shape now. At least in the front. Ted's office is still going to take some going through. Plus some of the equipment or tools are apparently misplaced. I'm wondering if they're in that black hole of an office."

Zelda launched into a description of everything she'd done to get both the mechanics' schedule, the customer schedule, and even the accounting books back into shape. I got the impression from listening to her that she ruled the garage with an iron fist.

Eventually, amazingly, someone did come over to rescue me. It was Grayson, and I was pretty sure he did it out of pity for me. I slipped away as Zelda engaged in an animated conversation with Grayson about the upcoming homeowner association meeting and some gossip about homes in the neighborhood that were not complying with one provision or another.

It was odd that Flora hadn't made it over. Things might get a little awkward if Reggie turned up since I wasn't sure how many people he'd know at the party. Also, I had to wonder what was going on. Flora wasn't one for standing people up. She was one of those extremely punctual people. Was her preoccupation to do with all the weight on her shoulders? Being part of a police investigation? Or could it be something more? I put the thought firmly out of my head.

I looked around my backyard to gauge if everything was going smoothly. There was plenty of food, which was good. Mona and Wilson were sitting next to each other in folding chairs and holding hands, which was even better. There was plenty of cheerful conversation going on and no one looked like they weren't being included. The only thing, to my eyes, that looked a little off was Jeremy and Augusta. He was talking with his friends, but was watching Augusta closely and, it seemed to me, with concern. And Augusta, in the fairly short amount of time that I was away, seemed to have downed a fair amount of alcohol.

Chapter Sixteen

I rationalized that Augusta might *not* have had a fair amount. It could be that she was just slow to metabolize it. She wasn't very big, after all. Regardless, it looked as if she needed to either slow down or come to a complete stop. I guessed that she was drinking because of nerves. I saw Jeremy approach her and ask if she'd like him to get her some water.

I didn't get to see the outcome of that because Grayson's two other friends came over to introduce themselves. He was still tied up with Zelda and gave me an apologetic glance.

It turned out, though, that I didn't really need rescuing because Lars and Norman were very easy to talk with. Well, Norman was, for sure. He was a big guy—the size of someone who might have played a defensive position in football. And he loved to talk, which made things much easier for me.

Lars was just about the polar opposite of Norman. He was nerdy with a high, academic forehead and a quiet manner. He was watching me thoughtfully as Norman talked.

"Great party," said Norman. "And you or Grayson did a fantastic job with the burgers."

"Oh, that was all Grayson," I said with a laugh. "You're lucky that I wasn't in charge of grilling. I'm much better with a stove than I am with a grill."

This made Norman launch into a soliloquy on grilling. He'd apparently grilled just about everything that could be grilled and possibly a few things that couldn't. The long list included blueberry cobbler, peaches with cinnamon, tofu, quesadillas, watermelon, and edamame.

"Wow," I said when he'd taken a breath. "Why aren't *you* the grill-master for this party?"

Norman grinned at me. "But Grayson is perfectly capable and did a good job."

Grayson was finally able to break away and joined us. "Hey guys," he said, sounding relieved at being able to escape from Zelda's clutches.

I said, "Norman was just telling us about his grilling skills."

Grayson rolled his eyes, teasingly. "I keep telling him he should write a cookbook. Has Lars even gotten a word in edge-wise?"

Norman looked a bit abashed. "Sorry, Lars. I forget how darned quiet you are."

Grayson told me, "You and Lars actually have quite a bit in common."

"Oh?" I asked politely, turning to the thin young man.

He gave me a crooked smile. "I have the feeling Grayson is referring to the fact that I also spend a lot of my time with books."

"Do you? What do you like to read?" I was surprised that I hadn't seen him at the library with all the other big local readers.

Lars glanced shyly at me. "You're probably wondering why I haven't been at the library much. It's because I'm big into marginalia."

Norman looked horrified. "Marginalia? That sounds illegal, man."

I chuckled. "It's a term for writing in the margins of books. It sounds like Lars is someone who likes jotting arcane notes in the margins and probably underlining or highlighting."

Lars gave me an approving look. "Both."

Grayson said wryly, "Well, it sounds like an expensive hobby, if you can't check out books from the library to support your reading habit. I've been in your house and have seen the stacks and stacks of books there."

Lars shrugged a thin shoulder. "It's not so bad because I hang out at the second-hand bookstore. I'm starting to think the guy who owns it is specifically searching for the kind of stuff I like to read at yard sales and flea markets because it's always available there." He smiled at me. "And, to answer your question, I like reading a variety of different stuff. My favorites change, but right now they're *The System of the World* by Newton, *The Age of Reason* by Paine, and *The Art of War* by Sun Tzu."

"Nothing like a little light reading," said Norman, still looking horrified. "I'll stick to my graphic novels, thank you very much."

Lars glanced over at Norman. "Graphic novels have gotten pretty deep, themselves. Lots of the classics have been made into graphic novels—I've seen a great one of *Moby Dick*."

Grayson said, "What really interests me are the puzzles Lars does."

"No sudokus for him!" said Norman. "And none of those 'spot the difference' picture puzzles."

"I mostly like logic puzzles, although the cryptic crosswords can be fun, too," said Lars.

I gave him a rueful look. "Okay, well, you've lost me there. I was doing fine with your reading list, though. It reminded me that I wanted to read *The Art of War* again."

Grayson asked me, "Ann, you always do a great job matching library services to patrons. Any suggestions for Lars?"

I thought about this for a second. "Well, I'd think it might be tough to find logic puzzles in a second-hand shop. At least ones that haven't been written on at some point. But we have a nice collection at the library, actually. You could always make a copy of the puzzles that interest you so you could write on them."

"Now that's a good idea. I have a printer at home that makes copies. I'll have to stop by the library and take a look," said Lars.

A few minutes later, Grayson made sure I was finally eating. I'd been so busy hostessing that I hadn't made time to actually eat any of the food that I'd prepared. As I ate, Grayson idly talked to me about his friends, giving me a little more background on them. Then he said, "Looks like you have another arrival. Maybe one of your patrons?"

I looked up and sure enough, Linus was there, clutching a small vase of flowers and looking a bit uncomfortable. I jumped up and hurried over to greet him.

"These flowers are beautiful, Linus, thank you! I didn't even think about decorating."

It was true. With all the cleaning and worrying and grocery shopping, I hadn't considered doing anything to make the party a little more festive.

He smiled at me as he handed them over. "They're all from my garden."

"Well, I can tell your garden is amazing. I'll have to come by and see it in person some day." Grayson walked up to join us and I added, "This is my friend, Grayson. Grayson, this is Linus. I can't remember if you've met."

They shook hands and Grayson said, "I don't think we have, although I've seen Linus at the library. Good to meet you."

Linus said with a smile, "I think I'm something of a fixture at the library." He looked around at the group of people and said, "Ann, thanks so much for inviting me here today. I just wanted to bring the flowers by—I'm afraid I can't really stay."

I knew that even dropping by and being surrounded by a big group of strangers was tough for him. He made my introversion look minor in comparison. So I said warmly, "Thank you so much for dropping by, Linus. It means a lot."

He colored a little from the compliment and then made his goodbyes. Although his departure was somewhat hampered by Fitz who, having spotted him, couldn't allow him to leave without giving him a little love.

After Linus left, I glanced around the yard, making sure everything was going well. Being a hostess of a fairly good-sized gathering felt like being a lifeguard. I was there to swoop down and help resolve any problems I ran into.

Fortunately, there didn't seem to be much to be concerned about. Zelda had poured herself a tiny cup of white wine and seemed to be speaking sociably with the neighbor who'd been avoiding her. From the relaxed look on the neighbor's face, Zelda must not be zeroing in on her favorite topic of homeowner association violations.

The only thing I saw that made me wrinkle my brow a bit was Augusta, who now appeared unsteady. I watched as Jeremy brought her a large cup of ice water and some food. Unfortunately, the food only served to make her turn a little green.

Grayson followed my gaze and said softly, "Is she okay? It looks like Jeremy is worried about her."

"I'm not really sure. Honestly, it looks like she's not feeling very well."

Grayson said, "Want to go over and check in?"

I did, so we joined Jeremy and Augusta where they were sitting in the shade. Jeremy looked relieved to see us.

"Is everything okay?" I asked in a cheery voice that didn't really sound much like my own.

Augusta gave me a bleary look. "Hmm?"

Jeremy said carefully, "We were just realizing that Augusta isn't feeling so great. I thought maybe I could drive her back to her place."

Sadly, Augusta immediately rejected this idea. She frowned at Jeremy and shook her head, her hair flying everywhere. "But I want to stay here." She looked at me and said, "Good party, Ann."

We stepped out of Augusta's earshot to continue our conversation. Jeremy gave me an apologetic look. "We came here separately. I feel like I need to make sure she gets back home all right."

He was being nice about it, but I could tell that Jeremy was done. He looked tired and like he just wanted to head back to his place and watch the football game by himself. I couldn't really blame him—he hadn't signed up for a first date where his date became intoxicated to the point of feeling ill.

I immediately said, "I'll drive Augusta back home as soon as the party is over."

Jeremy, again, looked tremendously relieved, but said, "Are you sure?"

I nodded. "It seems like she doesn't want to leave early, so if she's basically the last guest, she shouldn't have a problem going home. And, like I mentioned, I do know Augusta fairly well—she's one of my regular patrons at the library."

Jeremy, if possible, now looked even more relieved. "Oh good. I felt bad saddling you with a total stranger and felt bad for Augusta, too. That makes it easier." He paused. "I haven't had the best luck with relationships. And this one hasn't really started off on the right foot, either."

Grayson said, "She was probably just nervous and ended up drinking a little more than she was planning to."

Jeremy said, "I figured that was the case, too. Just the same, I don't think today went as well as either of us wanted it to. Anyway, thanks so much, Ann, for the party. It was really good to meet you."

"Good to meet you, too."

Jeremy told Augusta bye then quickly headed out. Grayson gave me a wry look. "It doesn't look like that date is going to blossom into anything else, does it? At least Mona and Wilson seem to be doing all right."

They definitely were. They were sitting together and quietly watching the proceedings while holding hands.

"That's a relief. I don't think I could have handled the tension below the surface at the library anymore."

A couple of people came up to thank me and head back home. After another thirty minutes, most of the guests had filed out—most likely because the game was going to start and they wanted to catch it at home.

Then Grayson, Augusta, and I were the only ones left.

Grayson said quietly, "Would you like me to drive with you? I could help walk her in and out of the car. In case Augusta stumbles or something?"

I shook my head. "Thanks, but I think when she's sober again later, that will just make her feel even more embarrassed. It's probably better if I'm the only one to take her home."

Augusta was, actually, dozing in her chair, her head slumped to her shoulder and her hand curled under her chin.

I crouched in front of her and said gently, "Hey. Augusta?"

There was no movement at all, just the tiny puffs of breath she took that blew strands of hair that had fallen in front of her face.

I jiggled her knee softly. "Augusta?"

Her eyes flew open with alarm this time and she looked around her with wide eyes as if trying to figure out where she was.

"It's okay," I said quickly. "Just wanted to let you know that my get-together has wrapped up. I thought I might help get you home."

Augusta dragged a hand over her eyes. "Is there any water?"

"Sure thing." She had water beside her, but I figured some cooler water might be more appealing. I handed it to her and she quickly gulped it down. She made a face afterward, though, as if her head or stomach or both were starting to bother her.

Grayson was watching from a short distance away, wanting to see how steady Augusta was on her feet.

It didn't seem to occur to Augusta that she might not be steady on her feet whatsoever. She stood up, wobbled, gave a wide-eyed look, and then plopped hard back into her chair.

She moistened her lips and said in a croak, "I might need a little help."

"Should Grayson give you a hand?" I asked, not sure how much help she might need.

Augusta shook her head decisively. "No thanks. I think if I can lean on you a little bit, that might work out."

The second attempt at standing went better. There was no crashing back down in the chair again. Augusta kept her hand on my arm and we made our way through my house and out to the front of the house.

I grabbed my car keys and Augusta and I climbed into my old Subaru. I headed carefully down the street in the direction of the library, which was close to where she lived.

Augusta suddenly seemed to remember some of what had transpired during the party. She groaned. "Jeremy?"

I kept my voice light. "He needed to get back home a little on the early side. He offered to take you back home but you wanted to hang out a bit longer."

Augusta groaned again. "Think I told you how bad my dates always went. Looks like I sabotaged this one, myself."

I carefully said, "Well, I think I might keep looking for another candidate. But Jeremy seemed to understand—he chalked it all up to the stress of the day. And I thought maybe you weren't really accustomed to doing much drinking."

Augusta gave me a wry look from the passenger seat. "That's really generous of you both. Sometimes I do drink too much, though. The problem is, when I *do*, it's like in the worst possible circumstances. Like a first date." She was slurring through her words, but seemed to be making a real effort to focus. She frowned. "Did I do anything to mess up your party?"

"No, no. Everything is fine." I gave her a reassuring smile.

"I'm really sorry," she said in a small voice. "I guess it was stress, like Jeremy was saying. But not just a date or even being around a bunch of people I don't know well. The whole thing with the murders has been awful."

I had the feeling that the regret she was feeling was really trickling in now but that it might be gushing in later on. I tried to keep things upbeat. "I bet it's been tough to deal with."

Augusta gave a rather wobbly nod that nearly hit her head against the passenger window. "I just feel bad about Jonas. I mean, I didn't kill him or anything, but I feel bad that he's gone. He wasn't such a bad guy, really."

I gave her another smile and didn't answer since I didn't feel the same way. "What were the things you liked about him?"

She gave a sleepy grin. "Oh, I don't know. He had a real sharp sense of humor and that was sort of fun."

"Sharp?"

"Yeah. Oh, wait. Maybe that's not really the right word. Maybe 'wicked' would be better. Sometimes he'd laugh but it might be at someone else's expense." Augusta shrugged.

Jonas sounded like he was a real charmer. It was a shame that Augusta's date today hadn't gone well because Jeremy definitely seemed to be an upgrade.

"I mean, he definitely didn't deserve what happened to him, even if he was a jerk." She was mumbling more now and I had the feeling she was going to drop off at any moment. "Neither did Ted. What's going on in town? Murders? The cops have got to keep on top of this."

"I'm sure they'll arrest someone soon," I said soothingly. Augusta had now suddenly vacillated from drowsy to agitated. I preferred drowsy.

"Poor Ted," she said. She was quiet for a few moments and I thought she might have nodded off. But then she said, "The last time I talked to him, he seemed like everything was going in the right direction for him, you know? He was always kind of dour, but he actually seemed *happy*. So sad."

I said, "It really is. Hey, I think we're coming up on your house. What was the house number?"

Augusta gave it to me, slurring again and I pulled into her driveway.

"I can get inside okay," she said as she pushed open the door. She stood up and promptly threw up into the bushes lining her driveway. Then she turned and gave me a sad look.

"You're okay, Augusta. Let's just get you inside and settled, all right? That will make me feel a lot better." I slung an arm around her and we made our way to her front door. She fumbled with the keys for a minute before giving up and handing them over to me. I unlocked the door and herded her inside.

"Would you like to sit up for a while?" I thought it might be a good idea instead of lying down.

Fortunately, Augusta agreed with me. "Mmm-hmm."

I settled her in a recliner in her living room and then set about finding a large tumbler of water to put beside her. Then I brought a trash can and set it next to her, just in case. By this point, she'd fallen asleep in the chair. I locked the door behind me and pulled it shut.

Chapter Seventeen

Grayson was still there when I got home. It looked like he'd taken advantage of the time by taking out the garbage, putting dishes in the dishwasher, and cleaning up the grill. He gave me a wry smile. "Everything okay?"

"I think she'll be fine. She did get sick once and I have the feeling that might have helped." I rubbed my forehead, feeling a small headache coming on.

Grayson gave me a hug. "It was a great party, Ann. Everyone seemed to have a good time and the guys really enjoyed meeting you."

I smiled at him. "I enjoyed meeting them, too. They're all so different from each other."

Grayson said, "I thought you might want to put your feet up for a while and just chill out, considering. How about if I just check in with you later?"

He was reading my mind, which I appreciated. At this point, nothing sounded better than curling up with Fitz on the sofa and either reading or taking a nap or both. "That sounds perfect, thanks. And thanks for clearing everything up—I really appreciate it."

After Grayson left, I refilled my water bottle and headed into the living room. I groaned when I spotted a purse with Augusta's initials on it sitting primly on an end table. There was no point in trying to give it back to her now, I figured. Better to let her get a nap in.

I settled on the sofa. There was something that was bothering me—something that Augusta said. I mulled it over for a few minutes, but couldn't put my finger on it. Idly, I picked up my laptop, thinking if I didn't force the memory, it might come to me.

I decided to google everyone at least tangentially involved with the murders. Hattie, of course, had quite an online profile, considering her position at the school. She'd also given a number of different talks, apparently, to other schools in other towns and some of those were online. I listened to some bits of those. They were mainly on active listening, empowering students, encouraging collaboration, and nurturing creativity as a method of innovation in the role of principal. It was clear that Hattie had goals beyond her principal position to be giving these talks and even keynoting at various education conferences. She had her own website, aside from the school's profile on her, with a tab that was devoted solely to the different lectures she could deliver. It looked like she definitely would have a lot to lose if her affair had been uncovered and there'd been a scandal.

Flora had a much smaller online footprint. She didn't seem to be on social media whatsoever, which was pretty unusual in this day and age. She was on the garden center's staff page and that was the only place I could really find her. She'd listed her hobbies as gardening and reading. It did seem like she and Reggie had a lot in common, despite the age difference between them.

Augusta's online presence was kind of a mess. She didn't have any privacy controls on her social media, so her profiles were open for anyone to see. After taking a look at them, I didn't think that was such a great idea. Her friends from college liked to post old pictures of them from their university and sorority days and some of them bordered on inappropriate. Lots of drinking, lots of boys . . . regular college fun. The only problem was that she didn't have the privacy settings turned on so anybody—like a prospective employer—could see everything on her profiles.

Then I looked up Reggie online. As expected, he had a picture on the college's faculty page. Apparently, he taught both upper-level courses and 101-level classes to freshmen, as he'd mentioned when I'd spoken with him. Out of curiosity, I looked up the boy that my patron, Denise, had brought up when she and Ramona were talking to me at the library . . . Steven Richards. His social media came up when I limited the search to the Whitby area, but it was all locked down so I couldn't see anything but his profile picture. I did recognize him, though, from around town. Besides his social media, the next thing that came up was an arrest record. I frowned, scanning the police record. Apparently, he'd been arrested for dealing drugs. A Schedule I drug. I looked it up and it seemed to be marijuana. Did this mean Reggie was a customer? Or was he tutoring Steven, as Ramona had suggested? Maybe Steven had been expelled from the college and Reggie was consulting with him on becoming re-enrolled.

I set the laptop aside and mulled over everything I'd read. There was still something that was bothering me from earlier, but it was frustratingly elusive. I decided it might come to me if I just did something completely different for a little while. I picked up my book.

Fitz, having been very social most of the day, happily leaped up to join me. He curled against my legs, purring, as I turned some soft music on my phone and started reading.

I read for about an hour and then the soft music and Fitz's warm body lulled me into a nap. I drifted off, thinking I'd be enjoying one of my twenty-minute snoozes. But when I woke up, the sun was starting to go down. I groaned. That was the kind of nap that was sure to mess me up when it was time for me to turn in.

Fitz stirred as I did, stretching his front legs out and giving a massive yawn before looking sleepily at me. I rubbed his head. "We got quite a nap in, buddy. It was probably a record for me."

Fitz always seemed to think I should take *more* naps, likely because cats sleep twelve to sixteen hours a day. One of his favorite things to do was to try and lure me into curling up with him by stretching out fetchingly on the sofa or the bed.

Then, like a bolt from the blue, the elusive bit of information that I'd been trying to access, came to me. Augusta had said "the last time I talked to Ted." But she'd said earlier that she didn't know Ted at all—that she'd never even met him on a professional basis because she hadn't brought her car to his garage. With all the alcohol she'd consumed, she'd totally contradicted herself. But was it because of a completely natural urge to cover up the fact she'd been acquainted with a murder victim? Or was it something darker?

Then Fitz jumped as my doorbell rang. I looked at my watch. It was probably Augusta, feeling a bit more sober and ready to pick up her purse. I reached for the doorknob warily.

Chapter Eighteen

I pulled it open to see Reggie there, smiling and looking hesitant as he held a bottle of wine. "Hi, Ann. I have the feeling I got the times for the party wrong." He gave me a rueful look. "Judging from how quiet it is here, I'm guessing it's all over."

"I'm afraid everybody has left and Flora never was able to make it by. Would you like to come inside for a minute? I've got tons of leftovers."

Reggie said, "Oh, I don't want to put you to any trouble. Plus, I ate recently. I always snack before heading out because I feel really awkward eating at parties."

I had the feeling that Reggie felt really awkward at parties, period. "Maybe a to-go bag, then? Seriously, you'd be doing me a favor."

"Sure. If it's not any bother. That would be great."

I ushered him in, thinking as I did that this must be a record about twenty times over for the number of people I've ever had in my house on any given day.

I gestured for him to sit down and headed into the kitchen to put a collection of food together for him. "Can I get you something to drink?" I was really getting good at the hostess duties.

"What? Oh, no. Thanks, though." Reggie settled down on my sofa next to Fitz and started aimlessly rubbing him as I put a bunch of food on a paper plate, wrapped it in plastic wrap, and put it in a bag for him.

I said, "Sorry you missed Flora. Have you had that coffee date we were talking about last time?"

"Not yet. I figured I'd just ask her to coffee during your party today." Reggie's voice sounded just short of pitiful.

"I'll have to check on Flora later. It's really not like her not to show up or give me a call."

Reggie said, "You're sure she's not seeing anyone, right? I mean, maybe she just started dating someone and you just haven't heard about him yet. She's been so busy with the house and yard that maybe she hasn't had the time to tell you."

Reggie clearly hadn't dated anyone for a while, judging from the anxiety in his voice. It sounded as if he wanted to make absolutely sure he wasn't going to be rejected or rebuffed when he asked Flora out.

"Do you know if she's seeing anyone?" he finally asked. "I've tried to look her up on social media, but it doesn't look like she's online. I was just wondering if you knew. Off-hand, of course."

"I don't believe she is," I said carefully. "If she's been too busy to tell her friends about a new relationship, she's probably too busy to get *into* a new relationship. You should probably ask her yourself, though."

He sighed. "I'm not very good at this. I feel like I'm in kindergarten and asking a friend if such-and-so likes me."

I chuckled. "Well, I was just thinking that it was pretty extraordinary that anyone would think of approaching me for any sort of romantic advice. If you were aware of my checkered dating history, you definitely wouldn't do it."

Reggie smiled at me. "Believe me, I totally understand and relate."

"To *me*, it seems like Flora is interested in you. But I think that's something you've got to figure out, yourself."

"Right. Right. Good point." He sighed again. "This stuff is terribly painful for me. I really couldn't be more awkward when it comes to dating. But I'm going to try to move forward and talk with Flora. What's the worst that can happen, right?"

"Exactly." I came back into the living room and handed him the bag of leftovers from the party.

My phone rang and I said, "Sorry, I should probably get this." I was thinking it was probably Augusta looking for her purse. But it was Zelda, instead.

Reggie started rubbing Fitz again as I took the call.

"Ann? This is Zelda Smith," came the crisp voice.

As if I knew so many Zeldas that I needed to distinguish between them. "Hi there."

"I took it upon myself to bring a stack of Ted's paperwork from his office back home with me," said Zelda. "And there was one thing I saw in the stack that I wanted to ask you about."

"You took paperwork *home*?"

Zelda sounded annoyed. "Now, don't fuss, Ann. I don't believe there was anything personal in there. No sensitive information. It all appears to deal with business. I suppose that's why the police didn't spend much time with it all."

"I was more thinking about it from the angle that you're doing work after hours, at home."

Zelda sniffed. "Needs must, Ann, needs must. Anyway, there's a purpose to my call."

Naturally. Zelda wasn't the one to phone for purely social reasons. Reggie took out his phone and was idly scrolling online.

"I was trying to call Burton, but he isn't answering his phone. Do you happen to know what the murder weapon was for Jonas's murder? There was some rumor around town that it was some sort of automotive tool."

I suddenly became a little more alert. Burton had said it was a torque wrench, which was why he'd originally considered Ted such a suspect.

Zelda continued impatiently, "Ann? Are you there?"

"Yes, I'm here."

Zelda said, "It's just that Ted made a note that he'd loaned a torque wrench to a Reggie Bartlett. This Reggie was a friend of his, I suppose. But it's the missing tool that the mechanics at the shop have been complaining about. It set off some alarm bells."

The same alarm bells that were ringing in my head. As calm as I could, I said, "Sorry, Zelda. I don't know anything about that."

Zelda sounded put-out. "Hmph. All right, then." She paused and then said gruffly, "Nice gathering today, by the way." And she hung up.

Reggie glanced up at me. "Everything okay?"

"Sure," I said in as breezy a tone as I could manage. "Sorry, I just think I'm just worn out from the party today."

"Sorry—of course you are. I'll get out of your hair. Thanks for the food."

Reggie leaned forward like he was about to get off the sofa and Fitz gave him a wary stare at all his excessive movement. But then he stopped short, peering at my laptop. Then he looked at me, a very serious expression on his face. I froze, my mind spinning trying to come up with a reasonable explanation for why I had a story about Steven Richards pulled up on my computer.

"That's interesting," said Reggie in a cool voice. "It's actually very coincidental that you would have been looking into Steven."

I shrugged, trying to look as casual as I possibly could, although I had the feeling my heartbeat might be able to be heard across the room. His reaction was pretty excessive if he just thought I was being nosy. This was more like he was afraid I'd discovered something he didn't want uncovered. "Do you know him? I was just speaking with a patron at the library who mentioned a friend's son had gotten into some trouble at the college."

"Really?" Reggie's voice was acidic. "Again, that's quite a coincidence. I guess reference librarians are all about uncovering things." He shifted so that he was now in a sort of crouching position.

I decided it was time to give up the pretense. Maybe I could just keep him talking until I could either grab my phone, run out the door, or both. "It's a coincidence because you obviously know Steven, don't you? And I have the feeling, judging from your interest in Flora, that you and Steven weren't in any sort of relationship. So that leaves the reason Steven was in trouble—drugs."

I couldn't read Reggie's face at all. All I knew was that any of the friendliness he'd shown earlier was completely wiped from his features now. Fitz was still eyeing him with concern from the floor.

I continued, "I don't even think these were really big-time drugs, were they? It looks like Steven was just a fraternity guy who was trying to make a little extra money on the side, selling to his frat brothers . . . and maybe a professor or two. You strike me as more of a pot kind of guy anyway. The problem was, though, that if it got out, you were going to lose your job, weren't you? Not only were you doing illegal drugs, but you were buying them from a student at the school you taught at. You wouldn't want to lose your livelihood, would you?"

Reggie stood up. "Where did you hear that little snippet of information? About Steven being connected with me?"

I shifted back a little bit. "I can't honestly remember. I sort of collect information as I go through my day. I talk with a lot of people."

"Yes," said Reggie thoughtfully. "I think that's what worries me. Your talking with people." He took a step toward me and I instinctively took one backwards, feeling like I had started in some sort of awkward dance.

He lunged at me and I scrambled off to the kitchen, Fitz bounding along beside me, clearly unhappy by the tenor of the voices he was hearing. Reggie grabbed for my arm, but I scooted around to the other side of the kitchen table. The errant grab knocked him off-balance and he fell forward on top of my small folding table, which promptly collapsed.

Taking advantage of this, I ran around past him toward the door and outside. It was about then that I started screaming like a banshee.

Chapter Nineteen

It was also about then that I mowed down Augusta, presumably there to retrieve her forgotten purse. She looked quite a bit more sober than I'd seen her last, but gaped at me in astonishment. A driver who seemed to be an Uber driver, was parked nearby, also gaping.

Augusta and the Uber driver weren't the only ones staring at me. Mrs. Harris from across the way was outside dumping a mop bucket and stopped what she was doing to come toward me. Apparently, I wasn't known in the neighborhood for histrionics.

At that point, Reggie came tearing out of the house. Augusta didn't know what had happened, but knew something was very wrong and that Reggie seemed to be the one behind it. She immediately took out her cell phone and dialed the police. Reggie, realizing the jig was up, took off in a completely different direction. And, since he was on foot with no car evident anywhere, he wasn't making a huge amount of progress.

Augusta, having reached the police, was now stammering trying to tell them where we were and what was happening. That's when old Mrs. Harris grabbed the phone from Augusta's hand and barked, "Come here at *once*! Reggie Bartlett is running in the direction of Azalea Way and he just terrorized my neighbor." She hung up with a hmmph and returned to her mop bucket.

In the end, Reggie apparently hadn't been very well conditioned for running. Nor did he likely have any thought-out plan for where he was going since he likely hadn't thought our visit was going to turn into attempted murder. At any rate, it wasn't long before I heard sirens in the background. Then, after very little time, the sirens stopped.

Augusta was peering at me with concern, likely reflecting the same expression I had used just hours ago for her. "Are you okay?"

I gave a scratchy-sounding chuckle. "I'm doing pretty well. My heart is pounding pretty hard, though."

"Let's get you inside and pour you something to drink," said Augusta. She added wryly, "Water for me, maybe something stronger for you. I'll send the Uber away and just call another one later."

While she was getting the drinks, I said, "I had a question for you, actually. Earlier this afternoon, you mentioned that you and Ted had spoken about something. But you'd said that you didn't know him at all."

Augusta returned with a glass of white wine for me. Her face was pink as she said, "Apparently, I was saying all kinds of things today. It's true—I did casually know Ted. Considering I'd already claimed a close connection with Jonas, I didn't think it would be a good idea for me to admit I knew a second murder victim, too."

Fitz was standing in my open front door, watching me with concern. He bumped his head lovingly against me as I walked up. I scooped him up and settled down on the sofa, where I promptly started shivering, despite the warmth of the little fur baby on top of me.

Augusta, who probably still felt pretty wretched, rallied enough to throw a blanket around me, bring me a tall glass of white wine, and pour herself an equally-tall glass of ice water. Then she set about calling Grayson, after getting his number from me.

Grayson apparently was very alarmed at hearing his girl-friend had just had some disturbing, as-yet-undisclosed en-counter with someone running from the law. Augusta tried to tell him I was just fine but he arrived while she was still talking on the phone to him.

Augusta seemed relieved at being able to dispatch her du-ties. "The other Uber is here. I'm just going to grab my purse and head out, Ann. Thanks again for everything today."

Grayson gave me a worried look. "Hey, what happened? I thought you were just going to chill out here for the rest of the day."

I gave a short laugh. "Well, that was the plan. Fitz and I were all cozy on the sofa when there was a knock at the door."

"And it was Reggie? He's that college professor who lives next door to Jonas's house?"

"Right. He didn't get the time for the party right, so he was there late. He was asking me questions about Flora, Jonas's sis-ter. Reggie is kind of shy but it was obvious from day one that he had a crush on her. He was asking me if she was dating anyone or if I thought he should ask her out."

Grayson rubbed his head, frowning. "Okay. Sounds innocent enough, even if it's kind of random."

"I know. I basically told him that giving advice to the lovelorn was out of my wheelhouse and that he should talk with Flora, himself. I got the impression he was trying to limit the possibility he was going to get rejected. He was asking me questions about Flora because he has low risk-tolerance."

Grayson said, "I guess he has low risk-tolerance in *that* situation. But it sounds like his tolerance is higher in others. Augusta was saying Reggie was the person who murdered Jonas and Ted?"

I shrugged. "It sure seems that way. Of course, he never seemed like he had that much of a motive—he was just upset with Jonas over various yard transgressions. But the real problem was that Jonas, who was an adept blackmailer, had figured out something about Reggie. Reggie had to get rid of Jonas or else he'd lose his job. He'd borrowed a torque wrench from Ted—who he *did* know, despite what he'd said—to work on his classic car. I guess he must have taken it over with him to Jonas's house, assaulted him, then wiped down the tool and tossed it into Jonas's garage."

There was a tap at the door and Burton stuck his head in. "How are you holding up?" he asked me after he'd greeted Grayson.

"Better now," I said with a smile. "Have you got some good news for us?"

Burton was now looking a lot less-stressed out than he was when I saw him at my party earlier today. "I do indeed. Reggie Bartlett is in custody. What's more, he's confessed to both murders. But then, I guess I shouldn't be surprised considering he couldn't think of a great excuse for why he was running from the cops. He did go into a few of the whys and hows, but before I run through those, I wanted to hear what happened on your end of things, Ann." He took out a small notebook and a pen.

Fitz moved slightly and mewed a hello to Burton who lightly scratched him under his chin before sitting down in a chair across from me.

I considered this. "I think I'm still just sorting it out. I was telling Grayson about it right before you came in. Reggie dropped by my house late for a party and looking for relationship advice. Killing me was the last thing on his mind right then."

"But something changed," said Burton.

"Reggie stood up and was about to leave. But he spotted my laptop and saw I had a page pulled up on a particular student at his college. The kid had recently gotten into trouble selling drugs."

Grayson grimaced. "And Reggie realized you'd had an epiphany."

I gave them a rueful look. "I guess I'm not much of an actress. I tried to persuade him that I'd been looking Steven up for other reasons."

Burton frowned. "Was this Steven Richards? That's the only student I remember us pulling in recently."

"Exactly. One of my patrons who knew *knows* the family mentioned Steven and that he'd been over at Reggie's house on a couple of occasions."

Burton jotted down some notes. "So Jonas made the connection, obviously, and tried blackmailing Reggie. Who probably would have had a lot to lose."

"That's right. Plus, Zelda had called me just moments before that and found a notation in Ted's office that he'd loaned a torque wrench to Reggie. I was on high alert already by the time Reggie saw my laptop screen. Anyway, once Reggie realized I knew what had happened, he was after me. I was able to get away from him and run outside the house, where I ran into Augusta. Literally." I shrugged. "And that's pretty much where we are now. So, from what I could see, it was just a case of Reggie having too much to lose, as you mentioned."

Burton said, "So you found out about Steven kind of randomly, it sounds like?"

I gave him Ramona and Denise's names. "I'm sure they're going to be delighted at being able to help you out—Ramona is apparently a big fan of police shows. They're neighbors of Reggie's and Jonas's. Ramona was talking about the stress of living on a street where a murder has happened. Then she talked a little about how Reggie seemed to be trying to flirt with Flora. Her mom, Denise, was there with her, though, and her mom was saying that she thought Reggie had 'a young man' and wasn't interested in dating Flora."

Grayson said, "So she'd noticed Steven coming and going and had drawn her own conclusions. But Steven was actually there delivering drugs to Reggie."

"Right. And I don't think they were even class-A drugs or anything—probably just pot. But that would have made Reggie lose his job, of course. Especially since he was buying the drugs from a student at the university he taught at." *where*

Burton tapped his pen on his small notebook. "But Jonas drew the *right* conclusion. And Jonas was always on the lookout for a way to get a little leverage on someone else. He realized there was something shady going on and kept an eye on it. Then he decided to blackmail Reggie like he'd blackmailed other people in his sphere."

I nodded. "But Reggie, for whatever reason, had a lot less risk-tolerance than the other people Jonas was blackmailing. He didn't want to lose his job, which would likely mean he'd lose his house. And it would probably mean a job change because he wouldn't be able to pass a background check if he had a drug charge. Considering there aren't that many jobs in Whitby, he'd probably have had to move. I guess he figured that it would be better to just get rid of Jonas completely. He also doesn't come across as someone who's swimming in money."

Burton jotted down a couple of notes and then tapped his pen against the paper again. "But Ted was wondering why Reggie wasn't getting the wrench back to him and why the police were so interested in it. We'd figured out it was likely Ted's."

"Right. And I have the feeling that Ted just wanted to give Reggie a chance to explain himself. Maybe Ted even thought that Reggie might be totally innocent. He was the kind of guy who didn't want to turn someone in if there was a reasonable explanation. The only problem was that there *wasn't* a reasonable explanation."

"Because Reggie had killed Jonas," said Burton grimly.

Grayson said, "That must have really scared you when he looked over at the laptop like that."

"It did. When he came to the door, I thought he was Augusta, coming back to get her forgotten purse. I wasn't really suspecting him of anything but keeping secrets at that point. I didn't know for certain that he was the one who killed Jonas and Ted. And he'd shown up with a bottle of wine and ready for the party"

Burton closed his notebook. "Well, to use a literary reference, all's well that ends well. Thanks to you, we've got Reggie locked up where he belongs. I'm just sorry he had to scare you half to death for that to happen."

"I think I'm recovering nicely," I said with a smile as Fitz yawned and stretched out on my lap in a manner that looked very awkward but was apparently exceedingly comfortable to him.

"I'll let you go—time to go have a talk with Reggie. It sounds like Flora had a lucky escape." Burton's face was stormy.

That she did. It was good that her budding relationship with Reggie hadn't progressed any further than it had. Which was just when my phone buzzed with a text message. Flora was full of apology—she'd been cleaning and thought she'd just take a short nap. Hours later, she woke up. She figured she'd been just catching up on sleep.

Burton headed out and Grayson looked at me with concern. "You've got to be totally exhausted, Ann. What a day."

"It was pretty good up until the last hour or so," I said with a smile. "Today went even better than I'd hoped it would. Maybe being extraverted is okay for short periods of time. Not only was the party a success, there's been an arrest for two murders."

"Enough to build up an appetite, I'm thinking," said Grayson. "Are you hungry? What with being a terrific hostess, you didn't leave yourself much time to eat at the party."

I thought about it for a moment and realized with surprise that I was actually starving. "A little food would be amazing." I hopped up. "I'll pull some things out of the fridge and we can have a feast here in the living room."

He shook his head and said, "Nope! I'll pull it out and put it on plates like a little buffet. I put it away, so I know where I've tucked it all away."

Grayson returned minutes later with steaming food, which he lined up on the coffee table in front of me. I heaped a plate full of leftovers and Grayson turned on some relaxing music on his phone for us to eat to.

I gave a happy sigh. "The perfect way to end the day. I love hanging out with you."

Grayson gave me a mischievous smile. "Even though you spent the day with other people?"

"I guess it's because you're not just 'other people.'"

Grayson said, "I feel the same way."

We were quiet for a few moments and then Grayson said, "I'm so glad you didn't end up getting hurt. I don't know what I would have done if you had."

He reached out for a hug and I relaxed into his arms.

The quiet of the house, the satisfying food, and the gently purring Fitz made everything else recede to the background as Grayson and I curled up on the sofa together.

About the Author

Elizabeth writes the Southern Quilting mysteries and Memphis Barbeque mysteries for Penguin Random House and the Myrtle Clover series for Midnight Ink and independently. She blogs at ElizabethSpannCraig.com/blog, named by Writer's Digest as one of the 101 Best Websites for Writers. Elizabeth makes her home in Matthews, North Carolina, with her husband. She's the mother of two.

Sign up for Elizabeth's free newsletter to stay updated on releases:

https://bit.ly/2xZUXqO

This and That

I love hearing from my readers. You can find me on Facebook as Elizabeth Spann Craig Author, on Twitter as elizabethscraig, on my website at elizabethspanncraig.com, and by email at elizabethspanncraig@gmail.com.

Thanks so much for reading my book...I appreciate it. If you enjoyed the story, would you please leave a short review on the site where you purchased it? Just a few words would be great. Not only do I feel encouraged reading them, but they also help other readers discover my books. Thank you!

Did you know my books are available in print and ebook formats? Most of the Myrtle Clover series is available in audio and some of the Southern Quilting mysteries are. Find the audiobooks here.

Please follow me on BookBub for my reading recommendations and release notifications.

I'd also like to thank some folks who helped me put this book together. Thanks to my cover designer, Karri Klawiter, for her awesome covers. Thanks to my editor, Judy Beatty for her help. Thanks to beta readers Amanda Arrieta, Rebecca Wahr, Cassie Kelley, and Dan Harris for all of their helpful suggestions and careful reading. Thanks to my ARC readers for helping to spread the word. Thanks, as always, to my family and readers.

Other Works by Elizabeth

M **yrtle Clover Series in Order (be sure to look for the Myrtle series in audio, ebook, and print):**
Pretty is as Pretty Dies
Progressive Dinner Deadly
A Dyeing Shame
A Body in the Backyard
Death at a Drop-In
A Body at Book Club
Death Pays a Visit
A Body at Bunco
Murder on Opening Night
Cruising for Murder
Cooking is Murder
A Body in the Trunk
Cleaning is Murder
Edit to Death
Hushed Up
A Body in the Attic
Murder on the Ballot
Death of a Suitor

A Dash of Murder
Death at a Diner (late 2022)
Southern Quilting Mysteries in Order:
Quilt or Innocence
Knot What it Seams
Quilt Trip
Shear Trouble
Tying the Knot
Patch of Trouble
Fall to Pieces
Rest in Pieces
On Pins and Needles
Fit to be Tied
Embroidering the Truth
Knot a Clue
Quilt-Ridden
Needled to Death
A Notion to Murder (2022)
The Village Library Mysteries in Order (Debuting 2019):
Checked Out
Overdue
Borrowed Time
Hush-Hush
Where There's a Will
Frictional Characters
Spine Tingling (late 2022)
Memphis Barbeque Mysteries in Order (Written as Riley Adams):

Delicious and Suspicious
Finger Lickin' Dead
Hickory Smoked Homicide
Rubbed Out
And a standalone "cozy zombie" novel: Race to Refuge, written as Liz Craig